CROWDED LAND OF LIBERTY

Also by Dirk Chase Eldredge

Ending the War on Drugs

CROWDED LAND OF LIBERTY

Solving America's Immigration Crisis

BY DIRK CHASE ELDREDGE

Bridge Works Publishing
Bridgehampton, New York

First North American Edition

Published by Bridge Works Publishing Company,
Bridgehampton, New York
A member of the Rowman & Littlefield Publishing Group

Distributed by National Book Network

Library of Congress Cataloging-in-Publication Data
Eldredge, Dirk Chase, 1932–
Crowded land of liberty : solving America's immigration crisis /
by Dirk Chase Eldredge.—1st North American ed.
p. cm.
Includes bibliographical references and index.
ISBN 1-882593-41-3 (alk. paper)
1. United States—Emigration and immigration—
Government policy. I. Title
JV6483.B53 2001
325.73—dc21
2001037771

2 4 6 8 10 9 7 5 3 1

Printed in the United States of America

MAR - - 2002

DEDICATION

This book is dedicated to Majken (Mickey) Johnson who has been my mother since I was nine. From that day to this, she has warmly welcomed me as her son and provided all the love, guidance, and support anyone could ask for.

This dedication comes with deep respect, love, and appreciation for all she has done for me.

CONTENTS

Author's Preface

In the course of its history, the United States has developed a vibrant, variegated population unlike any other country on earth. From our earliest immigrants, refugees from the British Isles who began arriving in America in 1607 to our latest, Cambodians and Senegalese, our nation has embraced and, in spite of instances of xenophobia, found room for all.

Descendants of the early Anglo-Saxons were augmented by northern and eastern Europeans. Accidents of history gave us the Irish beset by the 1840s potato famine and European Jews fleeing religious persecution. Today these Caucasian elements comprise seventy-two percent of our population.

Shamefully, most African-Americans and Blacks from the Caribbean and South America came here as slaves. But since 1868, when the Fourteenth Amendment to the Constitution of the United States granted Blacks full citizenship, our efforts to elevate this concept into real equality, though still marred by lingering racial prejudice, have produced heartening progress. Black Americans now comprise twelve percent of the population.

Asian-Americans (four percent of the population) first came in significant numbers from China as cheap labor needed to work California's gold mines and help build the transcontinental railroad. Legislation and popular prejudice caused citizenship to be severely restricted from 1882 until the late 1940s. But with three decades (1970s to the 1990s) of dramatic increases in Asian immigration, Asian-Americans have demonstrated their broad range of skills and entrepreneurship. Intermarriage is common, particularly among the Japanese, who marry outside their race about fifty percent of the time.

Hispanics — mostly from Mexico but amplified by many from Central and South America as well as the islands of the Caribbean — make up an energetic, motivated eleven percent of the American mixture. Intermarriage outside their group is also common, and currently between one-third and one-half of Hispanics marry members of other ethnic groups. The remaining one percent of our population consists of Native Americans and a fast-growing, mostly highly educated contingent from India and other near-eastern countries.

This, then, is America, a unique, inclusive blend of many races and cultures. We are, as we proudly tell the world, a nation of immigrants. Yet, it is obvious that recent immigration policies have brought crisis upon us, both physical and psychic, that previously did not exist. While we can readily acknowledge that immigration has played a priceless role in our country's childhood and adolescence, we are now a mature nation. Just as an individual's behavior, suitable during youth, may no longer be appropriate as an adult, our established nation now has different prerogatives and goals from its earlier years. As James Reston, the late, great *New York Times* columnist wrote, "The history of mankind is strewn with habits, creeds, and dogmas that were essential in one age and disastrous in another."

Uninterrupted economic growth is one of those creeds that has been a major cause of uninhibited immigration. From our agrarian beginnings, we have become a nation of cities, where most immigrants now cluster in unprecedented numbers, instead of spreading themselves evenly over our landscape. The problems of urban overcrowding and social friction are a recipe for endless, unnecessary civil strife, if not, ultimately, violence. When we ask ourselves, "What is our objective in bringing this crisis to our nation?" we find no answer. And why? Because immigration policies that brought about the status quo simply evolved with no plan or purpose.

Our unrelenting pursuit of economic growth has driven us to accept more and more immigrants. Worshiping at the altar of economic expansion has required ever more immigration acolytes. We need to learn there are more effective ways to improve our quality of life than by seeking the continuous, straight-line economic growth that has been America's Holy Grail. We need a nobler purpose than simply making more money than our parents. We must recognize that our country needs some breathing room. Where once we had vast open spaces to conquer and virgin prairies to till, we now have an unprecedented volume of urban newcomers, some with high fertility rates.

I reject any suggestion that I am racist, bigoted, or anti-immigrant. As one whose de facto mother from the age of nine is a wonderfully nurturing, Swedish immigrant, and who shares three of his grandchildren with their other grandfather of Japanese lineage, I say the United States needs no apologists for its population. But I am greatly disaffected by the present immigration policies of the United States. They are without thought or objective and do not serve our mature nation's needs. This book's purpose is to take an unflinching look at these ailing policies and propose constructive remedies.

D.C.E.

CROWDED LAND OF LIBERTY

"In an avalanche, each unique,
beautiful snowflake pleads not guilty."

— BENJAMIN ZUCKERMAN,
U.C.L.A. astronomer and environmentalist

1

Why a Crisis?

The United States, until 2000, was basking in the warm glow of prolonged economic growth and low unemployment. Mesmerized by the length and strength of the economic expansion, neither citizens nor our political leaders allowed the problems of unchecked immigration to register on their anxiety meters. Although economic history has shown us time and again that to predict a recession following an extended period of growth is akin to predicting one will exhale after inhaling, we seem unable to imagine what effect excess immigration will have during and after an inevitable downturn in the economy. No major candidate in the 2000 election even approached the subject of immigration.

Yet, millions of immigrants — legal and illegal — are inflicting a crushing burden on our already disadvantaged underclass with a flood of cheap labor. When the predictable recession comes, an avalanche of societal problems will thunder down, led by the weight of cheap immigrant labor reducing wages on already low paying, entry-level jobs. Additionally, enormous immediate and future population growth diminishes the quality of life for natives and immigrants alike, due to the twin scourges of overcrowding and the resulting environmental damage.

Our immigration policy was drastically changed in 1965 by amendments to the Immigration and Nationality Act. Opponents charged that the amendments would greatly increase immigration. But Senator Ted Kennedy, floor manager for the amendments, said, "Under the proposed bill the present level of immigration remains substantially the same." Senator Kennedy also asserted that, "the ethnic mix of this country will not be upset." Both statements have proved false. Before the 1965 amendments, the ethnic mix of immigrants matched closely the ethnic mix of our population. Since 1965, the mandated immigrant mix has nearly excluded Europe as a source. It favors, instead, Third World Hispanic and Asian countries, contributing an unprecedented high volume of offspring. With the addition of huge numbers of illegal immigrants that yearly grow larger, our population has increased far beyond anyone's expectations. Although it took from the dawn of human history until 1800 to reach a world population of one billion, and by 1960, of three billion, by 2000, world citizens numbered six billion, a 100% increase in forty years. Such enormous population growth and its accompanying pressures on poor countries has resulted in unprecedented numbers of desperate, poverty-stricken people immigrating to the richer countries like the United States.

During the decade of the 1960s the United States averaged just over 300,000 legal immigrants per year. Because of the 1965 amendments, by the 1980s immigration had doubled to about 600,000 per year. The 1990s saw the number of legal immigrants to the U.S. balloon to an average of more than 1,000,000 each year. Legal immigration hit a peak of over 1.8 million in 1991. This is the highest level of immigration in our nation's history, exceeding the previous record of just over 800,000 per year set during the initial decade of the twentieth century.

To these numbers of legal immigrants, it is estimated that undocumented aliens add 275,000 people to our population each year. These are divided between "visa abusers," who enter legally and simply overstay their visas (forty-one percent), and those who sneak across our long, porous borders in the dark of night, or use falsified documents (fifty-nine percent). The Immigration and Naturalization Service (INS) estimates that we are host to about five million illegals today. However, the 2000 U.S. Census estimates eleven million.

When assessing the impact of immigration, the point to keep in mind is that population is affected first by immigrants themselves, then by their offspring. The birthrate among women born in the U.S. has been declining in recent years. On the other hand, the birthrate among today's immigrant women ranges from 3.0 children to a robust 4.6 children, depending on ethnicity and education. For this reason, according to demographer Leon F. Bouvier, the post-1970 population growth is nearly all due to immigration. If fundamental changes to our immigration policies are not made soon, current immigrants and their children will add twenty-five million people to our already crowded metropolitan areas every decade for at least the next sixty years. This is the equivalent of adding the present population of California to America's already jammed population centers every thirteen years.

President Clinton shared this truth with the American people in his final State of the Union message delivered on January 27, 2000: "Within ten years — just ten years — there will be no majority race in our largest state of California. In a little more than fifty years, there will be no majority race in America." Whether one applauds or condemns this alteration of our ethnic makeup, few would argue against the premise that so fundamental a change should have been exhaustively debated prior to its implementation. No such public dialog took place concerning one of the most drastic demographic changes in history. The result will be an overwhelming social revolution.

The most obvious and immediate negative impact of adding large numbers of people to already overcrowded urban areas is on the quality of life and on the physical environment. That Americans now regard the environment as nearly sacred is evident when we see the size and the speed of growth of the Environmental Protection Agency (EPA). While new, as federal agencies go — founded in 1970 — it now accounts for a seventh of the staff and a third of the spending of the entire U.S. government regulatory apparatus. Yet, during the same time period the EPA and its budget were growing at such breathtaking rates, the U.S. was welcoming record numbers of immigrants. From an annual rate of immigration during the 1970s of about 400,000, the rate has grown to over one million.

It is shocking to realize that our government's environmental and immigration policies are working at cross-purposes, and the objectives of immigration policy are out of alignment with environmental realities. Richard D. Lamm, former governor of Colorado, wrote in 1999 that public policy and most of our institutions as presently structured assume unlimited resources and an infinite capacity to create wealth with no ecological limits. The resulting society, he said, is vastly different from a society that assumes environmental and ecological limits.

Although the present concentration of immigrants is in urban areas, this overcrowding negatively affects our cherished environmental beauty, as well. One of our most famous and important bodies of water is the Chesapeake Bay, a virtual inland sea that runs from Baltimore, Maryland, to Norfolk, Virginia. Only a decade ago the bay yielded two million bushels of oysters each year, today only about 300,000. The cities and suburbs of Baltimore and Annapolis, Maryland, and nearby Washington, D.C., along with countless towns and villages are on or near the bay's shoreline. Runoff from farms, lawns, and sewage plants, plus air pollution, have combined to convert much of the bay into a watery desert. The amount of oxygen-depleted "bad water" increased fifteen-fold between 1950 and 1980. There is no evidence of improvement since then.

Roy Beck, Washington, D.C. editor of *The Social Contract* magazine, wrote:

> After years of study, it appears that the single greatest problem for the Chesapeake Bay may be population growth in the bay's watershed, according to Christopher D'Elia, provost of the University of Maryland Biotechnology Institute. And the single biggest cause of population growth in the Washington, D.C.–Baltimore metropolitan area in the watershed is immigrants and their children. . . .
>
> Governments, industries, and individuals have spent billions of dollars since 1970 to reduce air pollution and water pollution to save the [Chesapeake] bay. But the federal government has undercut all those efforts by forcing — through immigration — continued intense population growth in the watershed.

In addition to devastating many other natural wonders such as Chesapeake Bay, the environmentally negative impact of immigration on villages, towns, cities, and vast metropolises across the length and breadth of America is enormous. Some specifics: Forty percent of our lakes and streams are not suitable for bathing or fishing. Thirty-five states are using groundwater faster than it is being replenished. The Endangered Species Act, passed in

Why A Crisis?

1973, listed 500 plant and animal species by 1988; by 1993 the count was 700. During that period, we admitted nearly seven million legal immigrants to a country struggling with its own ecology.

When interviewed for this book, Dick Schneider, chairman of the Population Committee of the Sierra Club, a California-based environmental organization, said, "Immigrants are no bigger contributors to that impact on the environment on a per capita basis than are natives. It is a combination of their arrival in such great numbers and their subsequent fertility that does the damage." Schneider pointed to energy consumption as an example. Energy consumption per capita has remained static, but the dramatic increase in population has driven up *total* energy consumption, depleting resources and further polluting the air we breathe. His observations, made in mid-2000, were prescient. California's early-2001 energy crisis marked by soaring electricity costs and rolling blackouts affirmed Schneider's observations. While none of California's political leaders has the political courage to mention immigration as a cause for high energy consumption, it is clearly a major factor. From 1997 to 2000, energy demand increased by twenty percent while generating capacity increased a mere one percent.

Nationally, the cost of being host to more than a million immigrants each year expands further by the need for additional, necessary infrastructure. Not only are additional schools and roads required, but also additional sewers, water, public recreational facilities, police and fire protection, hospitals, and many other taxpayer-funded services such as Medicare and welfare. While citizens recognize the need for these services, to most immigrants they are at once a miracle and a magnet drawing them here.

In the thirty years since 1970, the number of licensed drivers in America is up by sixty-four percent, reports the *Wall Street Journal*, and vehicle miles traveled have increased by 131 percent. Yet, during that same period, the nation's road mileage has grown by only six percent. Remember that deficit next time you are stuck in traffic. In 1999 the California Business Roundtable estimated that $90 billion to $100 billion would be needed over the next ten years to bring the state's roads and public works up to par. Perhaps they had heard the joke about the number and size of the potholes pocking California's streets. Some are said to be so large they are being stocked with trout.

The infrastructure problem is by no means limited to California. Nor have we yet seen the worst of it. Michael A. Pagano, professor of political science at Miami University of Ohio, writing in *Government Review*, warns that if history is any guide, city finance officers can expect the downside of the boom-and-bust cycle to raise its ugly head. He cautioned that concerns about crumbling infrastructure are more pronounced during times of economic recession.

In addition to the damage done to the physical environment, high levels of immigration also affect what we will call the psychic environment. How pleasant or unpleasant are our surroundings? When we seek the tranquility of open space, can we find it? Is it overrun with people or so distant that it's impractical? Are the billions we are spending on freeways and highways reducing traffic congestion or does population growth cancel out our efforts? As we sit immobile on interstate parking lots, do we not curse the endless stream of cars?

The loss of open space is real and serious. Across America, people seek to get away from the clamor of the city and move far enough away to enjoy the beauty of nature *and* get to it quickly. As Francis Emma Barwood told *Newsweek* about a popular development on the edge of Phoenix, Arizona, "The people who bought houses in phase one were told they'd be surrounded by beautiful lush deserts, but instead they're surrounded by phases two and three."

Loss of open space is by no means limited to the exodus from cities to suburbs. Man's innate desire to communicate with the wilderness is also threatened. In 1993, Congress opened up 353 square miles at South Colony Lakes in Colorado's Sangre de Cristo Mountains. Within two years it was so crowded that rangers considered limiting the number who could visit. In state and national parks near population centers, reservations and daily visitor limits are becoming more common as the nation's population grows.

Arizona and Colorado are struck by both edges of the immigration sword. The two states are popular destinations for immigrants, mostly from Mexico. In addition, they are common destinations for Californians fleeing the huge influx of immigrants into what is already our most populous, yet still one of our fastest-growing states. In 1999, Richard Schneider of California's Sierra Club wrote that over eighty percent of recent population growth in California is a result of immigrants and the U.S.-born children of recent immigrants. Schneider pointed out that California is now growing at virtually the same rate as India, 1.8 percent per year. This is much faster than the rest of the country (1 percent per year) and the world as a whole (1.3 percent per year).

Traffic congestion is the part of our psychic environment that affects us most on a daily basis. Anyone traversing the streets and avenues of Manhattan or the freeways of Los Angeles must either curse the traffic or possess the patience of Job. The Federal Highway Administration offers no solace, predicting in the mid-90s that congestion on our already crowded highways would quadruple by 2005. Inasmuch as eighty-five percent of America's households own one or more cars, the enormous growth in the number of motor vehicles can only be fueled in large part by population growth. Traffic congestion is, of course, only one result of more motor vehicles. Another serious consequence is air pollution. The two problems go hand in glove, as immigration expert Roy Beck has written:

> The fight against air pollution may be America's greatest environmental success story. Despite Herculean clean up efforts, however,

about forty percent of Americans live in metropolitan areas that still fail to meet some of the Environmental Protection Agency's health standards. How different would this statistic be if there were sixty-five million fewer Americans driving cars and using electricity? And it only gets worse. Each year the U.S. population grows by [over a million] people, most of them immigrants and the descendants of recent immigrants.

In addition to a clean, open environment, a quality education for our children in schools adequate in capacity to insure reasonable class size is a vital part of our nation's psychic environment. Today, America's schools are undergoing an unprecedented period of introspection. Everything about education is on the table: faculty quality, teaching techniques, physical plant, even vouchers to provide parents with options for schools. We need to add another question to this healthy mix: Should we continue to add legions of foreign students, the great majority of whom have limited English capability, to our already beleaguered education system? Beck's look at the New York City school situation helps answer that question:

> In the thirty-three overcrowded high schools of Queens, teachers must deal with sixty languages. And the immigrant flows change so rapidly, says the superintendent, that "the

languages we need this September will be different than the languages we'll need the next September." Immigration has so overwhelmed the schools in Washington Heights, Manhattan, that teaching is done in shifts. Rapid immigration has left the neighborhood crammed with twice as many children under twelve as lived there before the boom in immigration that began twenty years ago. Some 25,000 children share two school playgrounds because portable classrooms have covered all the rest. There are thousands of children trapped inside crowded apartments with nowhere to play. . . . High school dropout rates exceed fifty percent.

New York State is second only to California in the number of immigrants who settle there, 95,599 during 1998 alone.

So great is California's school overcrowding problem, the need to complete a new school arises each day to keep pace with growth. Exacerbating the problem are some enterprising Asian parents who, because they value education so highly, make arrangements for their children to live with friends or relatives in America and simply drop their children here to be reared and educated. This practice is so prevalent in Southern California, with its large concentrations of Southeast Asians, the term "parachute children" has been coined to describe them.

Why A Crisis?

The problem of overcrowded schools exists not only in California and New York, but in all states with a high immigration influx. Texas, for instance, needs to open two new schools each week just to keep up. The Houston, Texas, school system, with its close proximity to the border of Mexico, has a large number of Hispanics and is growing rapidly. In 1998, the system became embroiled in a heated controversy when it began asking for the parent's Social Security number or other proof of residency to enroll a child. Deputy Superintendent Faye Bryant said they "began to require affidavits this summer from parents who had no other proof of residency, such as a utility bill." Although the president of the Houston Immigration and Refugee Coalition charged that the practice "violates people's rights and intimidates immigrants who are not U.S. citizens," they are similarly "intimidated" and "their rights violated" everytime a traffic officer asks for their drivers' licenses or an immigration official their passports.

In 1998, the Loudoun County school district, near Washington, D.C., had a similar brouhaha. Like many districts across the country, it imposes tuition on students who are not residents of the county. Because the U.S. Supreme Court ruled in 1982 that states could not deny free, public education to illegal aliens and their children, the district cannot charge illegal immigrant students tuition. However, it does charge students who are on a tourist visa, viewing them the same as citizen-interlopers from surrounding areas. To differentiate between the two situations, i.e., illegal aliens and aliens here on a tourist visa, the district began requiring illegals to sign a statement of no visa. Predictably, this drew fire from an immigrant advocate's group. David Bernstein of the Immigration Rights Coalition of Greater Washington, said that such a statement has a chilling effect on enrollment because it discourages immigrant children from going to school. "This should be about education and not illegal immigration," he fulminated.

But immigration and education are inextricably intertwined. A 1993 Rand Corporation study of urban school systems with large numbers of immigrants found that in inundated schools, "Education failure is the norm for immigrants and natives alike. Fewer than one of two kids going into these high schools comes out employable." The Rand study concluded, "The size of the wave and the chaos of the situation are too great."

In our highly politically correct society, it is perilous to talk about such downsides of multiculturalism. Yet, in addition to other psychic problems, a deep-seated frictional component known as "hate crimes" has surfaced concurrently with the steep rise in immigration. While this type of crime is not inflicted solely on immigrants, they receive far more than their share. Unsavory instances abound — for instance, the distribution of hate-filled flyers aimed at Chinese-Americans in the summer of 1999, in San Francisco. The flyer was titled *What About Us Whites* and its message was painfully clear. It urged white people to "Rip them off. Spit on them. Flip them off, anything." Reflecting on the gravity of such inflammatory rhetoric, Diana Chin, executive director of a San Francisco Chinese civil rights group, said, "All sociological data show this is how violence really begins. This kind of campaign that dehumanizes a community creates an environment that's ripe for violence." Racism is abhorrent in any form and these pamphleteers are obviously ignorant and unstable. Nevertheless, Asians were singled out for hostility at a time when they constituted eighty-five percent of the immigrants admitted through the San Francisco port of entry. Overwhelming numbers cause many citizens to feel threatened.

South Florida is another psychic hot spot because of its massive influx of Cubans. Particularly provocative was the 1982 statement by the mayor of Miami, Maurice Ferre, an Hispanic, that, "Within ten years there will not be a word of English spoken — English isn't Miami's official language. One day residents will learn Spanish or leave." While the mayor's prediction has not materialized, an elderly English-speaking pensioner in Miami complained of hearing only "Spanish on the school grounds, Spanish in the hospital wards, Spanish on the bus, Spanish on the freeways, Spanish in the store and bank."

The handling of the celebrated Elian Gonzalez case is another example of immigration-related friction. Elian was the six-year-old boy who clung to an inner tube when the small boat on which he and his mother were fleeing Cuba capsized. After his mother drowned, Elian was picked up and brought to Miami, where his extended family began a campaign to keep him in the U.S. in spite of his father's pleas to return the boy to him in Cuba. The protracted battle over Elian caused havoc both in Washington, D.C. and Miami. Civil disobedience, including blocking traffic and defying police, was used by thousands of Cubans in Miami, leading to hundreds of arrests. The early morning raid by armed INS agents to deliver Elian from his Miami relatives to his father was an international incident reflecting poorly on all concerned.

Repeated clashes between the U.S. Coast Guard and Cuban boat people trying to land on Florida's shores and claim political asylum have strained relations between Florida natives and the Cuban-American population. As arrests are made, Cuban-American protests frequently resort to civil disobedience. After one such incident, an article by Andrea Robinson in the *Miami Herald* reported the outrage of some Miamians:

> Through e-mail, telephone calls, faxes to the *Herald*, and talk radio, hundreds of non-Cubans were angered by what they see as an unlawful, self-defeating tactic of disrupting traffic.
>
> Although we have compassion for refugees ... Pushing the Cuban flag in our faces, screaming and blocking traffic is a poor way to say "thank you."

Why A Crisis?

These vignettes are examples of the hostility resulting from high levels of immigration. Immigration-caused friction inevitably leads to a crisis of anxiety among those whose turf is invaded. Recently retired dentist, Dr. Leon M. Ellis of La Cañada-Flintridge, California, tells of the transformation of his up-scale Los Angeles suburban community into "Korea Heaven." Local real estate professionals report that seventy percent of all residential inquiries now come from Koreans. Said Dr. Ellis, "Korean immigrants frequently buy single-family residences and turn them into a home for two or three families." He witnessed the community change from a quiet, homogeneous town to an overwhelmingly foreign enclave.

Wausau, Wisconsin, whose name and location seem to literally define "middle America" went through a metamorphosis which began in the mid-1980s as a generous experiment in multiculturalism. A well-intentioned few in Wausau reached out to some Laotian Hmongs, inviting them to resettle there from their war-torn region. What developed created another case of immigration indigestion. Roy Beck wrote:

> But much has changed since 1984. The number of Southeast Asians burgeoned, and the city's ability to welcome, nurture, accommodate, and assimilate the larger numbers shrank. . . .
> On my visit to Wausau, I found some anger. But the overwhelming emotion seemed

to be sadness about a social revolution that the community as a whole had never requested or even discussed. While most residents spoke well of the foreign residents as individuals, they thought that the volume of immigration had crossed some kind of social and economic threshold. Many sensed that their way of life was slipping away, overwhelmed by outside forces they were helpless to stop.

Beck believes that the higher the volume of immigration, the higher the sense of threat and resulting tensions.

Alexis de Tocqueville, in his 1835 classic, *Democracy in America*, warned we would have a difficult and resentful underclass when the slaves were freed. He was right. And how blindly we now repeat the tragic result of slavery, this time with under-educated, often illegal immigrants who are outside the mainstream of America.

The Rand Corporation, reporting on a 1996 study that *did not* differentiate between legal and illegal immigrants, had this to say about the economic progress of recent immigrants:

Immigrants [on average] have very low wages, and the evidence suggests that their wages will not improve substantially throughout their working lives. This evidence, combined with the fact that more-recent immigrants have had lower (age-adjusted) wages relative to earlier immigrants has substantial ramifications for public-service usage and tax revenues into the future. As well, the trends indicate that the economic and social divisions within the communities may be exacerbated.

Other studies agree with Rand's conclusions. Both the educational level, and even more important, the value that some immigrant families place on education are declining. The problem is particularly acute among immigrants from agrarian cultures. Such societies often place the immediate income-producing capabilities of school age children above the long-term value of education. From heavily Hispanic Washington High School in New York City comes a report from Carol Contos, an English teacher there for thirty years. On a typical parents night she says she may see the parents of seven of the sixty students she teaches. Her colleague, Francesca Burack, when asked how many parents call or come in to see her about their children answers, "Almost none." Parental involvement is a vital element in academic success, so it's little wonder that the national Hispanic high school drop-out rate is fifty-five percent compared to twenty-five percent for Blacks and thirty percent for Whites. Lack of education, low wages, and poor prospects for improvement spell underclass, and as our immigrant population swells, the underclass grows apace.

Vernon M. Briggs, Jr., professor of human resource economics at Cornell University, writes that if mass and unguided immigration continues, it is unlikely that there will be sufficient pressure to incorporate these groups into the mainstream economy. Instead, it is likely, he writes, that the heavy but unplanned influx of immigrant labor will serve to maintain the social marginalization of many African-Americans and Hispanics. As a result, he concludes, the chance to eliminate once and for all the underclass in the U.S. economy will be lost—probably forever.

During the 1990s and the first year of the new millennium, Americans enjoyed the longest period of sustained economic growth in our history. It is easier to ignore overcrowding, overpopulation, violence and deletion of natural resources during boom times. But when the recession phase of the boom-and-bust economic cycle arrives, not only will the infrastructure problems worsen, but also higher unemployment and falling wages will diminish further the physical and psychic components of this country's quality of life. The inevitability of these events adds to the urgency of corrective action in our immigration policies.

2

Good Intentions Gone Awry

History can help us understand the weaknesses of our current immigration policies. Starting with the passage in 1790 of the first federal naturalization legislation, our immigration laws followed a racial bias. The 1790 law required those naturalized to be "free white persons." In 1882, the Chinese Exclusion Act was passed in response to what many considered to be excessive Asian immigration. During the 1920s, legislation was passed to reduce immigration and to insure that emigrés followed closely the ethnic mix of the citizenry, again a more or less racially based approach.

In 1965, in its haste to correct past racial inequities in immigration policy, Congress passed amendments to the Immigration and Nationality Act of 1952 (The Act). This legislation was meant to change the focus of immigrant selection from country of origin, (and consequently, to a large extent, selection by race) to family unification, a process of uniting families in the home country with a legal immigrant in the U.S.

The Act divides us into two classifications; citizens and aliens who can be either immigrants or non-immigrants. Examples of non-immigrants are tourists,

21

students, and business visitors, and others who plan to be here only temporarily. They must leave after a specified time, which varies with their classification. No limits are imposed on the number of non-immigrants admitted in any one year.

Legal immigrants are those who seek admission to become permanent U.S. residents. Once admitted, they may stay and work forever. After five years they have the option to seek citizenship through naturalization.

In order to be admitted as a legal immigrant, a person must fit into one of four basic programs, all having an annual numerical limit. The first, and by far the largest of these programs, admits immigrants based on the objective of family unification. A subset of this program is labeled "immediate family." An immigrant qualifies for this program if he or she is the spouse or minor child of a U.S. citizen, or the parent of an adult U.S. citizen, and can be admitted immediately and without numerical limitation. Under the entire family unification program, 535,771 immigrants were admitted in 1997. Typical of immigration patterns of the 1990s, this was sixty-seven percent of total immigration for the year.

The troubling part of these statistics is not that nuclear families (spouses, children, and unmarried sons and daughters) are immigrating as a unit; they should. The weakness is that when the extended family (siblings and adult sons and daughters) are added to the already numerous nuclear family, the result is that about two-thirds of all immigration is based solely on far-reaching family relationships.

The second of the four basic programs, also subject to numerical limits, is employment-based immigration. Immigrants under this program are admitted based on their job skills or their ability to create jobs. Waiting times for these immigrants range from a few weeks to as much as eight years, depending in part on their classification. In 1997, a typical year recently, only eleven percent, or 90,607 immigrants were admitted under this program. To provide maximum benefit to the U.S., this group should comprise much more than eleven percent of total immigration.

"Diversity" immigration drives the third program. In 1990, Congress created this program in a belated and controversial attempt to reduce the dominance of Latin America and Asia as recent sources of immigrants. It was used by 49,374, or six percent of immigrants in 1997. This category should be eliminated. What is important is what immigrants bring to our country, not where they come from, or to whom they are related.

The fourth program covers refugees. This program admitted fourteen percent of all immigrants, or 112,158 people in 1997.

An additional one percent, or 10,468 immigrants were admitted in 1997 under various other minor programs, for total immigration that year of 798,378 new residents.

To illustrate the profound impact the 1965 amendments had on both our ethnic composition and the number of immigrants, consider that from 1820 to 1967 Europe and Canada accounted for eighty-nine percent of our immigrants, while Asia, Latin America, and the Caribbean produced ten percent. From 1968 on, Europe and Canada fell to about seventeen percent, while Asia, Latin America, and the Caribbean rose to eighty percent.

The numerical limits imbedded in the 1965 amendments are routinely exceeded due to a convoluted system of amendments and exceptions. The Act specifies that annual immigration should range from 421,000 to 675,000, depending on admissions the previous year. However, legal immigration has exceeded the lower figure every year since 1965. The top five countries of origin for 1997 immigrants were Mexico, 146,680; the Philippines, 47,842; China, 44,356; India 36,092; and the Dominican Republic, 24,966.

What is apparent from these bald facts is that we have a hodgepodge of conflicting agendas compromised into a policy without national purpose. Instead of a lively public dialog over the vital issues of the number and composition of future immigrants reflecting the will of the people, legislators have pursued their own objectives, large and small, noble and ignoble.

Immigration law is clearly more important to the electorate than some obscure tax law affecting only a portion of the populace. Determining the number and composition of those with whom we share our country, its schools, freeways, parks, hospitals, and neighborhoods, are territorial issues closest to every American's heart. These factors make immigration a highly personal issue, far more personal than who will be our next president, and one that should be openly discussed and dissected, not decided in the cloakrooms of Congress.

One would imagine that since immigration is so vital to each of us, promulgating laws about it deserves the most far-sighted attention possible. Instead, decisions are made in an expedient, politically charged atmosphere. On the side of increased immigration, we have those who profit from the lower cost of labor it provides. Historically, this has included food growers and processors, some manufacturers, restaurants, hotels and others who have come to depend on low-cost, unskilled labor.

Recently, some high-tech manufacturers have joined them, and, along with software companies, make the dubious claim that the U.S. is not producing enough programmers and engineers to meet their needs. They plead that we must allow in more immigrants to keep us competitive in today's global economy. The real reason for their plea is a desire to bring in foreign technicians who will work for far less than American citizens.

Allied with these forces, whose real agenda is to enhance their bottom lines, are scores of organizations whose collective agenda is to bring in as many family members and countrymen as possible. The agenda of these groups focuses solely on family reunification and constituency building.

Recently added to this chorus of open-door voices is big labor. After decades of opposition to increased immigration, in the spring of 2000, the AFL-CIO surprisingly announced its support for the idea of another general amnesty for the illegal immigrants we now host. By INS estimates, this will add six to seven million more illegals in the U.S. to the 2.4 million illegals granted legal status as a result of the 1986 amnesty, a grand total of nine million permanent U.S. residents who have been rewarded for breaking our immigration laws. Why this switch by big labor? It sees all those grateful, suddenly legal immigrants as a bonanza of new, dues-paying union members.

The rapid growth and effectiveness of Hispanic and other pro-immigration organizations has spawned an increase in ethno-centric members of Congress, who are indebted to their constituents.

James G. Gimpel and James R. Edwards, Jr., in their book, *The Congressional Politics of Immigration Reform*, write,

> Because worker's rights and civil rights have become intertwined in the 1990s, both Black legislators and their Hispanic and Asian colleagues from districts with large immigrant

populations see business as their common enemy. The Black, Asian-Pacific, and Hispanic Caucus organizations in Congress can therefore justify a united front, voting cohesively in favor of efforts to increase the availability of immigrant visas for purposes of family reunification, in favor of amnesty for illegals, and against efforts to restrict immigration.

This type of ethnic division bodes ill for the process of effective, purposeful immigration policy making. It's ironic that Black and Hispanic citizens suffer more than other ethnic groups by increased immigration, yet their leaders are among the most vocal favoring it.

An example of reason giving way to prejudice and political expediency was the long-running battle over the Simpson-Mazzoli Bill, which, after defeats in the Ninety-Seventh and Ninety-Eighth Congresses, became the Immigration Reform and Control Act of 1986, a compromise bill. Those favoring reduction of immigration conceded the granting of amnesty to the millions of illegal immigrants in the country at the time, in exchange for the concept of employer sanctions, which were supposed to deter future illegal immigration. It turned out to be a lose-lose bargain. As 2.4 million illegals became legal and began to initiate the chain immigration made possible by the family reunification policy, the sheer weight of these numbers began the slow slide of quality of life issues. And the idea of imposing sanctions on employers who hire illegals never worked because of the failure of enforcement. A study of the effect of immigration laws reported in the *San Francisco Chronicle* in October 1998 said that imposed sanctions on employers who hired undocumented workers had practically no effect on keeping illegal immigrants out of the labor market. Employers were not required to verify identification documents, so thousands of illegal migrants obtained work by presenting counterfeits.

The Fort Worth Texas Star-Telegram reported in April 1999 that:

> Employers say they are prohibited, though, from challenging all but the most obviously counterfeit documents — a measure that was put in the law to protect legal immigrants from discrimination but that can also be used by employers as a shield against penalties. "So, employers are walking a tightrope," an immigration attorney said. "If a person produces a driver's license and a Social Security card, and it *(sic)* appears to be reasonably genuine, then you have to accept it."

Additionally, the amnesty provision of the Simpson-Mazzoli Bill sent the message to would-be illegal immigrants everywhere that they should come to

America by any means, and hang on until the next amnesty. And — stranger than fiction — open-door advocates are already planning, with the support of the AFL-CIO, the next mass amnesty for the five to six million current illegals.

Surveys have shown that the public's wishes are being ignored on all aspects of the immigration issue. *The Congressional Politics of Immigration Reform* reports that a "June 1986 poll on immigration taken by CBS News and the *New York Times* . . . shows that in the midst of the legislative action on immigration in Congress that year, support for increasing immigration was uniformly low." A similarly worded 1994 study conducted by the same organizations showed support to be even lower.

Later, in the same book, the authors report on yet another study showing the flouting of the public's wishes. They see, from across all demographic and attitudinal categories, more support for decreasing immigration in 1994 and 1996 than in 1992. And in 1994 they find that even majorities of Hispanics and Asians support reduced immigration, as did liberals and those in nearly every other demographic group.

The ever-increasing flow of immigrants has not gone unnoticed. A *Times-Mirror* Center poll in 1994 indicated that eighty-two percent of Americans think the United States should restrict immigration. A CBS/*New York Times* poll two months earlier found only a six percent difference among those identifying themselves as Democrats, Republicans, or independents; all overwhelmingly objected to current immigration levels. Most citizens have generally positive attitudes about immigrants as individuals, the poll stated, and concluded it was the **number** of those individuals arriving each year that has overwhelmed many communities.

Congressman Lamar Smith, (R-Texas) former chairman of the House Subcommittee on Immigration, adds a coda to the poll. "Twenty years of polling research have shown that Americans consistently want to reduce both legal and illegal immigration."

An especially egregious instance of the frustration of the public's will occurred in California in 1994. Californians, in an effort to staunch the flow of illegal immigrants into their state, decided to take the step of cutting off public support for illegal immigrants through the referendum process. "Why," they asked, "if we are a nation of laws, should we taxpayers subsidize those who are here illegally?" Passage of Proposition 187, as it was called, would deny illegal immigrants access to public services, public schools, and non-emergency health care. A majority of fifty-nine percent of California voters approved the measure. Quickly after its passage, all three major Latino advocacy groups, the Mexican-American Legal Defense and Education Fund (MALDEF), the League of United Latin American Citizens (LULAC), and the National Council of La Raza (NCLR), joined other pro-immigration forces to thwart the proposition, which never became law. After a long legal battle, the proposition heaved its dying breath at the hands of the new governor, Gray Davis. The *Los Angeles Times* reported the demise of Proposition 187 on July 29, 1999, stating that the proposition had been approved by nearly sixty percent of California voters, becoming a national symbol of anger about illegal immigration. The *Times* forecast that the deal-killing seemed certain, according to the lawyers, to ignite additional controversy, since it would permanently bar enactment of the ballot measure's core provisions — those preventing illegal immigrants from attending public schools and receiving social services and subsidized health care.

Unfortunately, the U.S. Supreme Court had already ruled, in a 1982 case, Plyler v. Doe, that for a state to deny children of illegal aliens access to public education, Congress would have to pass legislation granting states that prerogative. Congress later tried, in 1996, to pass the so-called Gallegly Amendment that would allow the states this power. Senators Edward Kennedy (D-Mass.) and Alan Simpson (R-Wyom.) led the fight in the Senate against the measure. It lost 34 to 60.

3

The H-1B and Its Discontents

Black educator Booker T. Washington made an impassioned plea to a large group of industrialists in 1895 to hire American Blacks instead of depending on immigration to man their factories. He told a story of a lost and desperate sea captain finally sighting a sail and signaling the other ship of his plight. He had no fresh water on board; his crew was in danger of dying from thirst. The friendly ship signaled back that the captain should, "Cast down your buckets where you are." Certain they had misunderstood his message, the frantic captain repeated it several times. Each time the reply was the same, until finally he ordered his crew to comply. To everyone's astonishment, they brought up buckets brimming with fresh water. The ship was in the 200-mile plume of fresh water from the mouth of the Amazon River.

Hi-tech executives would do themselves and the nation a favor by embracing Washington's analogy and casting down their buckets to utilize American workers of all races rather than adding further to our nation's population.

Close to eleven percent of the visa allocations each year go to immigrants who have job skills in short supply here. The high-tech industries have successfully lobbied Congress to augment this category with supposedly temporary visas to fill alleged shortages, particularly of engineers and computer programmers. These are called "H-1B visas." The idea was sold to Congress on the basis that recipients would leave when the six-year term of the visa expired. It is patently obvious that most recipients will not want to leave after an investment of six prime years of their working careers, during which they are exposed to the charms of the United States.

Linus Torvalds, a Finnish H-1B visa holder and chief architect of the computer operating system, Linux, said to a House of Representatives field hearing, "Coming here we didn't know what to expect — whether we'd actually like living in the United States or not. Having been here three years I can definitely say we've liked it a lot, and we feel this is home."

Nor will their employers want them to leave. Digital Equipment Corporation's immigration manager, Patricia McDermott, admits that when the six years expire, her company will sponsor about half of their H-1B workers for permanent residence. It's a good bet that much of the other half will either employ the best available immigration lawyers to help them achieve permanent status or join the millions of illegals who have quietly and permanently overstayed their temporary visas. The INS estimates that forty-one percent of illegal immigrants initially entered the country legally as temporary visa holders and simply stayed.

The U.S. really loses in two ways with the H-1B
program. First, we award to a citizen of another country
an opportunity available to a U.S. resident, and second,
we add unnecessarily to our already excessive population. Of course, American employers must certify to the
INS that no U.S. resident can be found to perform the
work for which the H-1B immigrant is being recruited.
But there has been a constant effort by high-tech
employers to increase the number of H-1Bs. The program started in 1992 and admitted 50,000 skilled
foreign workers. By 1999 the flow had increased to
115,000 per year. As a result of the consistent hue and
cry for ever-higher quotas by the powerful high-tech
lobby, legislation passed in October 2000 increasing the
annual quota to 195,000.

James Grover, head of the Department of Electrical
and Computer Engineering at Kettering University in
Flint, Michigan, and Paul G. Huray, professor of
physics and engineering at the University of South
Carolina, wrote in 1998 about the H-1B program
which was then fifty-seven percent of today's size:

> Oh no! Congress is talking about an "engi-
> neering shortage" again. Whenever the econ-
> omy heats up, or when the United States is
> perceived to be militarily or technologically
> challenged, leaders who would otherwise
> trust the free market see doom . . . When
> Congress increased skilled immigration by

> more than 100,000 annually in the late 1980s,
> the number of unemployed engineers nearly
> doubled. Real engineering salaries dropped to
> a 20-year low by 1993.

America does not need more immigrants, even skilled workers, to compete with our own for the precious resources of jobs and opportunity. We are far better off to train citizens to fill these needs. Granted, this approach takes longer, but it allows nationals to move up the ladder of employment rather than have an immigrant capture that next rung. Representative Ron Klink, a Democrat from Pennsylvania, has complained that H-1B is a loophole for big companies to hire cheap labor. He calls it a huge loss to American workers, especially young people who have made their educational decisions based on a future job expectation. Instead, he believes, companies will be hiring cheaper foreign talent.

It is more than a self-serving assertion that the real motivation behind H-1B is cheaper labor. A 1993 national survey of college alumni revealed that an astonishing eighty percent of computer science graduates had gone into other professions, strongly suggesting that the function of the free market was being upset by external forces. If the invisible hand of the market were left to regulate wages within computer science, unfettered by a ready supply of immigrants, qualified workers would not be leaving the field in the midst of the information technology explosion.

In newspaper accounts of the H-1B controversy, there are recurrent references to cost cutting made possible by hiring foreign technicians. A March 1998 story in the *Washington Post* reported that some workers claimed the labor shortage is only a sham. They say employers are flooding the market with foreigners to keep wages down and to avoid hiring workers who lost jobs during previous layoffs and tend to be older and have higher wage demands. Later in 1998, the *Post* reported that Norman Matloff, a computer science professor at the University of California at Davis, had testified before Congress that foreign high-tech workers are paid fifteen percent to thirty percent less on average than Americans. And in the same year, *USA Today* called the labor shortage "a manufactured crisis." It cited statistics showing a seventeen percent unemployment rate for programmers over 50, those who command the highest salaries.

A month later, *USA Today* carried another story about an Indian electronics engineer named Mahesh Maddury saying, "I would have had to go back to India," had he not received his H-1B visa. That would have been a serious blow to him because jobs requiring his skills there are rare and pay "$3,600 per year v. $60,000 in the U.S." Mr. Maddury's situation helps explain why forty-four percent of the H-1B visas are granted to technicians from India. That India has some of the finest technical schools in the world, and its students an excellent command of English encourages huge numbers to desert their own country and emigrate to America, thus undercutting American labor.

No one denies that periodic shortages of specific technical skills occur in nearly every U.S. industry. However, increased immigration is the easy, faulty answer. Training Americans to fill our needs is both practical and preferable, yet a recent study funded by the Alfred P. Sloan Foundation and published in *Backgrounder* reveals the reason that's not happening:

> There is a remarkably lopsided incentive system that produces ever-growing numbers of alien Ph.D. candidates in science and engineering and smaller numbers of American candidates . . . For example, spending six or seven years of hard work (but little or no cash) for an American Ph.D. in science or engineering as well as an American green card is a remarkably attractive deal for a bright alien student. The similarly able American student willing to undergo some graduate training . . . can usually in much less time become a lawyer or an M.B.A. (or with a little more time, an M.D.), leading to a much higher income . . . than a Ph.D. So, fewer able Americans take on the grueling years of graduate study in the sciences and engineering, and more aliens do so.

What a condemnation of our educational establishment! Obviously, higher education is doing very little right. A two-hour drive from Silicon Valley is the University of California at Berkeley, arguably the most prestigious of the ten-campus statewide system, which boasts over 31,000 students, one in twelve of whom are foreign. A whopping eighteen percent of its graduate students are student-visa-carrying foreigners. Over 1,000 foreign graduate students are employed by the U.C. system as research assistants in government-financed research projects. (The spirit of the temporary student-visa program is that students will return to their homeland after graduation. How many do is a matter of conjecture.) In 1999 the congressional watchdog agency, the General Accounting Office, published a report showing that the University of California system billed the government $14,500 per year in waived tuition for each foreign assistant, and only $4,400 for graduate assistants who were U.S. citizens or green card holders. In addition, the U.S. paid the U.C. system $4,848 per year for each foreign research assistant in its Ph.D. program, compared to $2,322 for American students. U.C. does not contend it costs more to educate aliens than citizens. It simply has taken advantage of loosely-written federal guidelines to extract a little more money from the U.S. Treasury. Consequently, the U.C. system and presumably other university systems involved in government-funded research favor foreign graduate students as a means to increase their revenue.

The H–1B and Its Discontents

While no laws are broken, two important questions emerge: First, why should U.C. or any other university be paid a bonus, courtesy of U.S. taxpayers, to educate foreign students, and second: Why can't these bonuses be made available to citizen students?

Both the educational establishment and business are failing to serve our nation's best interests with respect to immigration. Expanding the pool of computer professionals by a policy encouraging broad use of aptitude tests to find potential programmers and systems engineers would create more opportunity and provide a path for talented new people and those in the lower echelons of high-tech companies to move up. International Business Machines built its early sales and systems staffs with just such an approach. When experienced programmers didn't exist, I.B.M. found trainable people with the aid of aptitude tests. Using this approach, it built a sales and systems organization so successful it dominated the computer industry from the mid-1950s through the mid-1970s.

Republican Senator Alan K. Simpson of Wyoming identified the real motives of both employers and employees, when he responded to those opposing his 1996 bill reducing H-1B visas:

> The computer industry is saying my bill will deny them the opportunity to get these highly skilled people to come to the United States.

They bring them here on temporary [H-1B] visas and who wouldn't work for one-third less as long as they knew at the end of the tunnel was a green card?

His bill never saw the light of day.

A widely used argument in favor of ever more immigrants, H-1B types or otherwise, is their track record of starting many new enterprises, creating more jobs "for the benefit of all." *The Economist* magazine, in its October 1999 issue, praised this presumed immigration benefit, "Silicon Valley is full of bright immigrants willing to sacrifice their ancestral ties for a seat at the table; almost 30 percent of the 4,000 companies started between 1970–1996, for example, were started by Chinese or Indians." One wag described these entrepreneurs as "silicon implants."

The conventional wisdom of this entrepreneurship as an overall benefit to America needs rethinking. First, the creation of a company occurs to fill a need in the marketplace; failing that, the company's life will be short and disappointing. If an immigrant does not fill the need, a current resident will, and the U.S. marketplace will have allocated the opportunity to one of its own rather than squandering it on a newcomer. Unless one assumes immigrants are somehow superior in their ability to recognize and successfully fill the needs of the marketplace, and no evidence supports that thesis, Yankee ingenuity and management ability are alive and well; just ask our competitors around the world. It is true that 30 percent of Silicon Valley's companies were founded by immigrants, but that says more about networking and the dearth of opportunity in other countries than it does about superior entrepreneurship.

"Opportunity" is the operative word. Stephan Gotz-Richter, president of TransAtlantic Futures Institute, and Daniel Bachman, the institute's chief economist wrote:

> They [Asian immigrants] often arrive here as graduate students and have little inclination ever to head back home. . . . Evidently equity ownership has global allure. And, for now, there's only one place where it is really possible to start your own company and get rich: America.

Why not reserve those opportunities for Americans? Some answer that immigrants *are* more entrepreneurial. An analysis released in early 2000 by the Center for Immigration Studies, a Washington, D.C. think tank, encouraging lower immigration levels declares that, according to census data, the once valid reputation of immigrants as more entrepreneurial than our population at large is obsolete. The Center found that in the past immigrants were indeed significantly more entrepreneurial than natives, but that the immigrant advantage had disappeared. In statistics from 1960 and 1997 that were quoted, the self-employment rate of immigrants fell from 13.8 percent to 11.3 percent, while the self-employment rate for natives increased from 9.6 to 11.8 percent. By 1997, the Center concluded, the presence of immigrants had no effect on the overall level of entrepreneurship in the U.S.

After laying to rest the shibboleth of immigrant entrepreneurship, Congress should take note and encourage education to promote native high-tech employees and employers. The crutch of low cost immigrants could be replaced easily with the sturdy feet of our own human resources.

A win-win alternative to importing more and more workers for high-tech industry at home is already in place by some software companies utilizing world-shrinking, newly economical, and sophisticated communications capabilities. A March 7, 2000, *Wall Street Journal* article tells of programmers halfway around the world performing complicated tasks:

> Software start-ups rely on technical help from experts in India, Eastern Europe, Turkey, and elsewhere. Novosoft, Inc., [of] Houston, [Texas] provides 250 programmers working in Novosibirsk, Siberia. Timescape, a custom-software developer based in Australia and Los Angeles, has used as many as 10 Siberian pro-grammers for six months. They're paid a quarter of what U.S. programmers make, don't get benefits and can be easily reduced or

increased in number, says Nicole Macdermott, vice president of marketing.

Of the 34,000 employees of software giant Microsoft, many are foreign nationals working in their own countries. Local workers learn every aspect of the business from translating software to marketing and sales. According to a Microsoft spokesman, the company has added more than 100 local software developers in India and Israel, and set up research facilities in China and England. While this approach denies Americans these jobs in favor of local hirees, it provides Microsoft with an employment cushion of remote resources while it deals with a *curable shortage* of homegrown high-tech workers in the U.S. Instead of trying to be the world's schoolhouse, all industry in the U.S. can emulate Microsoft by dedicating their educational resources to the training of our own citizens, while encouraging other countries to learn high-tech skills that can benefit their own economies.

In our higher-education system, another problem surfaces. Stories abound of eager and qualified American students being denied admission to their college of choice. Education resources are finite, thus the more seats we fill with foreign students, the fewer there are for our own citizens and legal, permanent residents. When a student is competing against his own countrymen, *plus* the cream of the crop from much of the rest

43

of the world, the law of probabilities erodes his chances. In addition to diminishing his chances for admission, foreign competition raises the question of fairness. Why should a qualified, motivated U.S. student need to compete with students from all over the world for admission to a school that was built by and for Americans? Additionally, state universities are built and supported with taxpayer funds. So we have the irony of a U.S. student denied access to the school of her choice while her parents subsidize the education of the foreign student who took her place. Foreign student enrollment in U.S. institutions of higher education in 1998 was estimated at 500,000 and growing.

Since space is not going begging in our colleges and universities, with a higher percentage than ever of U.S. high school graduates going on to higher education (from forty-six percent in 1960 to sixty-seven percent in 1998), all the more reason for these institutions to concentrate on accepting citizen students.

Race should not be a consideration in college admission; national origin should be. That foreign students can compete for our finite educational resources on an equal footing with American citizens and legal, permanent residents is illogical. That we squander educational opportunities on foreign students, given the nation's need and desire to increase opportunities for our minorities, is unwise. It is our responsibility to invest in our own.

4

Down on the Farm

High-tech firms are not alone in their sometimes unhealthy reliance on imported labor. America's agriculture industry has dithered for decades over a lack of workers for its unique labor requirements. On one hand, growers need large numbers of workers for short periods of time; on the other hand, they refuse to provide wages and living conditions that will attract and retain American workers willing and able to migrate from crop to crop. As a result, U.S. agriculture has come to rely on a continual flow of immigrants, most of them illegal, working for sub-standard wages. This economic aberration has allowed agriculture to perpetuate an economically synthetic situation.

Born and raised on a dairy farm, Manuel Cunha, Jr., of Fresno, California, has lived with the farm labor problem all his life. His home is in the heart of the verdant San Joaquin valley, which stretches north from Bakersfield to Stockton, in one of the richest agricultural areas in the world. Although of Portuguese descent, Cunha is president of the Nisei Farmers League (NFL) headquartered in Fresno. Comprising more than 1,000 member-farmers, the NFL was organized in

1971 by second-generation Japanese farmers. Today, it consists of a cultural cross-section of farmers throughout the San Joaquin valley. The NFL's mission is to advocate on behalf of its members for better farm labor, irrigation, and other matters of vital concern to farmers.

Says Cunha, "One of the primary reasons for passage of the Immigration Reform and Control Act of 1986 (IRCA) was to provide a permanent, stable agricultural work force." The Act legalized 2.7 million illegal aliens, from all walks of life, *plus* one million migrant farm workers. Members of the general illegal population were granted legal status if an individual had continuously resided in the U.S. since January 1, 1982. Those who had illegally worked on the nation's farms were designated as special agricultural workers, or SAWs.

Many of the would-be SAWs resorted to fraud under a provision of IRCA that provided legalization if they could show at least ninety days of farm work in 1985 and 1986. Many illegals claimed they had been paid in cash and thus had no records to prove their employment. In a classic example of naive legislation, they were then granted ninety-day work permits by Congress, supposedly enabling them to contact their former employers and obtain a confirmation of status. Border patrol agents trying to confirm prior farm employment joked about questioning one applicant on the correct way to pick strawberries. She replied that she got a ladder, climbed it, and picked the berries off the strawberry tree.

Mr. Cunha says that, contrary to what he and the farmers hoped, eighty-five to ninety percent of the legalized SAWs soon left farm work in favor of more desirable, permanent, full-time employment. Growers estimate that today's San Joaquin valley farm labor force is once again seventy to eighty percent illegal immigrants.

The IRCA legislation created the Commission on Agricultural Workers to review the effects of IRCA, and especially its SAW provisions. It made some startling discoveries. First, the commission established that the flawed worker-and-industry-specific legalization program was "one of the most extensive immigration frauds ever perpetrated against the U.S. government." Second, the commission found that although the SAW program legalized many undocumented farmworkers, the continued influx of illegal workers prevented newly legalized SAWs from obtaining better wages and benefits. Third, the commission reported that the farm labor market continues to leave the average farmworker with below-poverty-level earnings.

In spite of these failures, yet another illegal alien amnesty program is being considered by Congress. Because two powerful forces — the AFL-CIO seeking new union members and farmers still seeking cheap labor — back the program, passage in some form seems likely. Under this proposed amnesty, agricultural workers would have to log at least 1,040 hours or 180 partial days of work per year for five years to qualify for the coveted green card. While this new proposal sets the bar higher for legalization, IRCA demonstrated that the illegal alien amnesty is, at best, a five-year band-aid on the farmworker problem, not a long-term solution. The estimated 800,000 illegal farmworkers in the U.S. today will doubtless follow the footsteps of their earlier breathren on the path through temporary farm work and on to better-paying, easier, full-time work in other industries.

There is good reason for fleeing agricultural work. According to *Poverty Amid Prosperity,* "Relative to the average worker, farmworkers in the mid-1990s have lower take-home pay than they did in the mid-1960s." In short, market forces are thwarted by economically synthetic circumstances. What we should have instead is a workforce paid a wage that rewards the difficulty and physical demands of its work, a wage that compensates farmworkers for the necessarily transient nature of their work as they follow the ripening crops across the "fruited plain." But to achieve acceptable living conditions, farmer's cooperatives and farm labor unions must join in providing fair wages and housing at a fair price instead of lobbying for more and more bodies.

Testimony to the abysmal state of farmworker housing is provided by the recent $21 million settlement of a farmworker's suit charging housing discrimination in California's Riverside County. It is the largest farmworker fair housing settlement in the history of the Department of Housing and Urban Development and will doubtless serve to turn up the heat on the issue of farmworker housing across the country. Riverside is ranked number ten nationally, among counties, in agricultural production. As in the days of *The Grapes of Wrath,* a May 23, 2000, *Los Angeles Times* article reported that, "[E]very season workers flocking to [nearby] unincorporated desert communities such as Thermal, Mecca, and Oasis must sleep along roadsides or in trailers without indoor plumbing." There are countless other examples of despicable living conditions among farmworkers in what has been labeled "America's harvest of shame."

It should be emphasized over and over again that we have created an economically unsustainable farm labor paradigm by refusing to allow free market forces to establish farm labor wages and working conditions. We pay unrealistically low prices for fresh fruits and vegetables made possible by a system imposing poverty-level wages and often inhumane working and living conditions on a work force kept powerless by a competing stream of mostly illegal workers. Illegals are willing to work for nearly any price, under any circumstances, to avoid starvation. At the same time, consumer apathy, fostered by low prices for fruits and vegetables, aids and abets the status quo. Higher consumer prices may seem onerous, but are the only fair way to support our agricultural workers and provide a fair return for farmers.

Restructuring the economics of America's fresh fruits and vegetables is surprisingly achievable and not nearly as economically serious as generally imagined. A 1993 study showed that the average family's yearly expenditure for food eaten at home was $2,700, of which $270 was for *fresh* fruits and vegetables, the commodities whose harvest is most likely to employ immigrant labor. (Fruits and vegetables to be canned or frozen are mostly picked by machine.) Growers received twenty-one percent, or $57 of this annual retail expenditure. Farm labor, including supervision, typically represents about one-third of the farmer's cost of production for fresh fruits and vegetables. Therefore, the average consumer unit of 2.6 persons in 1993 spent $19 on farm wages and benefits for fresh fruits and vegetables. By extrapolation, if farmers doubled farm wages and benefits for fresh fruits and vegetables, it would add only 37 cents per week to the average family's food costs. None would disagree that this is an infinitesimal price to pay for ridding the farm workers of their ongoing plight.

And there is reason for optimism. Higher wages and prices could trigger appropriate Yankee ingenuity. An example of just such ingenuity resulted when the *Bracero* (Spanish slang for worker) Program that had supplied cheap Mexican tomato pickers for twenty years expired in 1960. Soon equipment developed that cut the tomato vine, shook off the tomatoes, placed them on a conveyor belt, sorted them by color as they moved past an electric eye, and deposited them on a truck. Reporting that result, Philip L. Martin, Professor of Agricultural Economics at the University of California, Davis, in his essay, "The Endless Debate," wrote that in 1960, a peak of 45,000 workers, eighty percent of whom were braceros, were employed to handpick 2.2 million tons of tomatoes for ketchup, grown on 130,000 acres, whereas in 1996, about 5,500 workers were employed to drive machines harvesting and sorting almost twelve million tons of tomatoes from 360,000 acres — a record crop.

Concurrently with the ending of the Bracero Program, the director of the California Department of Agriculture testified that, without braceros, "We could expect a fifty percent decrease in the production of tomatoes," compelling Professor Martin to conclude, "Farm wages in relation to farm machinery prices remained low throughout the bracero era, rose sharply in the 1960s and 1970s, and then began to fall as illegal immigration increased."

Professor Martin cites another example of necessity being the mother of invention among growers, this time in the sugarcane fields of Florida:

> [T]he Florida sugarcane industry began importing Caribbean workers to hand cut cane in 1943 and maintained that cane harvesting could not be mechanized because

unique muck soils would bog down machines. But after a lawsuit was filed in the early 1990s alleging that workers guaranteed $5.30 an hour and required to cut one ton of cane per hour should be paid $5.30 a ton, rather than the $3.70 a ton they were paid, cane companies mechanized the harvest within three years.

Naturally, there will be some economic dislocations as agriculture and other industries wean themselves from underpriced immigrant labor and adjust their economic structures to a new reality. Some prices will rise; some industries will require structural changes.

For example, the long-established practice of growing high priced, labor-intensive crops such as tree fruit, strawberries, and grapes in California's fertile San Joaquin Valley needs reassessment. During 1999, and continuing in 2000, Fresno County, located in the middle of this land of fruit and honey, suffered an average annual unemployment rate of fourteen percent, with three towns *averaging* over thirty-three percent. All this, while the state of California, and indeed the whole nation's, unemployment rate hovered around four percent.

Several factors such as the seasonal nature of agricultural work, the valley's low cost of living and pleasant ambiance compared to urban alternatives serve as magnets for the indolent, and the proliferation of false documentation used to "qualify" for social services, encouraged by lax enforcement of immigration and welfare laws, cause this unemployment anomaly. Thus, the area is nearly totally dependent on immigrant labor to harvest its labor-intensive crops. Philip Martin, agricultural economics professor at nearby University of California at Davis, describes the valley's raisin grape harvest as "the single most labor intensive [agricultural] activity in North America."

In an interview with raisin grape grower Mard Davidian, 64, of Kingsburg in Fresno County, he said, "The $6,000 per acre cost of converting my ninety-acre vineyard to an automated harvesting format would be difficult to recover in my farming lifetime." According to Davidian, both his age and the size of his vineyard are typical of the area, and he says he is almost totally dependent on immigrant labor.

But Davidian is nearing the end of his working life. Younger growers could move away from hand-picked crops to those more amenable to mechanization and reduce their dependence on immigrant labor. Fewer available immigrants, both legal and illegal, would also give a much needed boost to the grower's incentive to automate the harvesting of some crops. The raisin grape market and many others would also need to raise their prices in order to pay fair wages, provide decent living conditions for the workers, and return an adequate profit to the grower after paying for his automation.

U.S. farmers have grown accustomed to depending on cheap immigrant labor. Continuation of lax border security and guest worker programs simply perpetuates this reliance. They hold wages unrealistically low, stifle incentives to develop laborsaving harvesting equipment, and perpetuate the growing of crops that could not otherwise support themselves in a free market. If a U.S. farmer cannot produce a particular crop while providing decent wages and living conditions and sell it profitably at a competitive price, he should leave its production to someone who can, perhaps in another country. This is how the free market efficiently allocates its resources.

The answer to the question, "Are these objectives worth the price?" lies in public policy priorities. The objective of a more enlightened public policy would be to improve the lives of those Americans at the bottom of the economic ladder while controlling explosive population growth. To perpetuate subsidies of the wrong crops by exploiting mostly illegal labor is bad economics and inhumane public policy.

5

Chain Immigration Perils

> Who would call in a foreigner — unless an
> artisan with skills to serve the realm, a
> healer, or a prophet, or a builder, or one
> whose harp and song might give us joy?
> — *The Odyssey*

This quotation suggests a brilliant theme for restructuring our immigrant selection process. As Homer said over 2,000 years ago, immigrants should be admitted based on what they will contribute to the realm. To strengthen any entity — a team, a school, a company, or a country — first seek those with needed skills, not those whose main qualification is a family relationship. Except in matters of inheritance, nepotism has never been widely admired as a selection device. Why should it guide us in immigration?

The authors of the 1965 amendments to the U.S. Immigration and Nationality Act came up with the nepotistic concept of family reunification to show the world our immigration policies were free of the pollutant of discrimination against any nation or race. Roy Beck has discussed the motives:

> Conservative Democrats . . . feared that [the] proposal to remove the national origins quotas would flood the United States with immigrants from the Third World. They came up with something of a trick that would allow the United States to say that it had no quota discrimination against any country but which, in actuality, would bring about the same mix of immigrants as had been coming. The trick was "family reunification." While the reformers had wanted a priority on picking immigrants by skills, the conservatives insisted that the priority be on an immigrant's family connections to Americans.

Trying to look good while feeling good, conservative Democrats helped create an immigration policy with results a far cry from intentions by failing to admit that immigration policy is inherently discriminatory and can't be otherwise. Unless a nation throws open its borders and admits all comers, it discriminates against those it turns away.

Implying that family reunification as the central theme of immigration policy was based largely on misplaced sympathy, Peter Brimelow, author of *Alien Nation*, maintains, for instance, that immigrant families are little more disunited geographically than many American families, whose own adult children are often scattered around the globe.

Chain immigration, the empowerment of the primary immigrant to obtain preferential treatment for relatives — in effect, the ability to buck the immigration line — is a self-perpetuating result of family reunification and has a profound effect on population growth. Most Americans believe that a million new immigrants means one million more bodies. In fact, it means the addition of those one million souls, *plus* a variable number of relatives the original immigrant can sponsor into the U.S. via family reunification.

By 1981, some members of Congress recognized the serious problems that resulted from the 1965 amendments, so they created the Select Committee on Immigration and Refugee Policy, with Father Theodore Hesburgh, then president of Notre Dame University, as chairman.

Reporting to Congress that he feared family reunification would seriously swell the stream of immigrants, Father Hesburgh wrote:

> To illustrate the potential impact, assume one foreign-born married couple, both naturalized, each with two siblings who are also married and each new nuclear family having three children. The foreign-born married couple

may petition for the admission of their siblings. Each has a spouse and three children
who come with their parents. Each spouse is a
potential source for more immigration, and so
it goes. It is possible that no less than eighty-
four persons would become eligible for visas
within a relatively short period of time.

Ramiro Lamas and his five siblings dramatically illustrate the phenomenon of chain immigration. They are
among about 100 immigrants from the village of
El Salvadore, in Mexico's state of Jalisco, who have
settled in Juneau, Alaska. Ramiro resides there with his
Mexican-born wife and their four children, the eldest
born in Mexico, the others here. Lamas followed a trail-
blazing older brother to America, and like his sibling,
originally an illegal. After a stint in northern California
working in a mushroom nursery at below minimum
wage, Lamas and about three million other illegals
were granted legal status by the government's 1986
amnesty. Newly secure in America, he moved to Alaska
and now earns $18 an hour, plus benefits, as a school
custodian. Lamas's main reason for moving to Alaska is
significant: "In California the bosses know they can pay
you less, because there are twenty people from Mexico
looking for the same job." The oldest Lamas brother,
the first illegal immigrant of the family, brought about
the immigration of four other siblings and many prog-
eny. Ramiro Lamas and his wife became a family of six

in less than a dozen years, producing about twice the number of children as that of a typical native-born family.

A 1990 study for the National Committee for Research on the 1980 Census by Drs. Guillermina Jasso, a sociologist, and Mark R. Rosenzweig, an economist, both recognized experts on immigration, revealed that from the cohort they studied, one million immigrants sponsored somewhat more than an additional one-half million of their relatives. In an interview with the author, Dr. Jasso emphasized that today's immigration wave is much more Hispanic and Oriental than the largely European cohort they studied. She concluded that because Hispanics and Orientals have much larger families than Europeans, the multiplier today is considerably larger.

Today's multiplier is probably closer to the Lamas brothers' experience than the extremes of either Father Hesburgh or Drs. Jasso and Rosenzweig. The saga of the Lamas brothers tells us that America's immigration crisis is not limited to California, Texas, Florida, and New York; it is nationwide. A generation ago, who would have foreseen an enclave of 100 or more Mexicans in Anchorage, Alaska? According to a 1997 *Los Angeles Times* article, this is only one of many unlikely venues. The article tells of other budding Mexican villages in rural Maine; the Carolinas; Walla Walla, Washington; Northwest Arkansas; Atlanta; the Midwest; and from Atlantic City to Las Vegas.

Crowded Land of Liberty

In 1980, Cecilia Lucatero came to Southern California from Tijuana, Mexico, on a tourist visa but with every intention of staying. She did, and in 1986 married Max, also an illegal Mexican immigrant. That same year, amnesty made them both legal residents. When asked about chain immigration in an interview, Mrs. Lucatero told of a friend who also came to the U.S. illegally, was pardoned by the same 1986 amnesty, and subsequently sponsored his parents, a sister and a nephew. One amnestied illegal became five legal immigrants.

Like a delayed-action bomb, chain immigration is wreaking its havoc with population density, and perhaps our economy, long after the fact. It took Ramiro Lamas about a dozen years to grow from one immigrant to six. If we multiply the Lamas family and the friend of the Lucateros by millions, we can see that the full impact of laissez-faire admittance to the U.S. will be demonstrated by their children, Hispanics who will outnumber by far other ethnic groups in years to come.

Our immigration backlog as of January 1995, more than 3.7 million foreigners waiting to enter the United States, is only the tip of the iceberg. Almost all the backlog was for the family reunification category: 1.6 million adult brothers and sisters, 1.1 million spouses and children, and 500,000 unmarried adult children.

But the issue of immigration continues to be on auto-pilot, and its inevitable impact will not be truly understood until the coming of a recession. By then it will be too late. Too late to implement the kind of policy that immigration expert Professor George J. Borjas called for in his op-ed piece in the April 2, 1999 *New York Times*, ". . . a policy that pays more attention to fiscal consequences and to the economic impact on those at the bottom rung of the economic ladder."

Furthermore, recent studies show the educational level of the average legal immigrant is dropping, and we can safely assume the drop among illegal immigrants is steeper. U.S. Bureau of Census figures for 1999 show that ten percent of natives are high school dropouts as opposed to 33 percent of recent legal immigrants. The figures also show dramatic changes in poverty levels for today's immigrants compared to those of 1970. Then, thirty-nine percent of immigrants who had arrived in the previous ten years lived in or close to poverty, as did thirty-five percent of natives. By 1999 their comparative situations had dramatically changed; fifty-four percent of recent immigrants lived in or near poverty, compared to twenty-nine percent of natives.

Professor Borjas and others have expressed concern over the declining skill level of today's immigrants and their disproportionate participation in various welfare programs. Borjas has written "that more recent immigrants are more likely to receive cash benefits because later immigrant waves are relatively less skilled than earlier waves." The primary reason for this decline in skills is immigration policy focused on family reunification, rather than on the potential for productive contribution.

. . .

As an early step toward putting America's self-interest first in our immigration policies, we must put a humane end to the practice of chain immigration. After a 24-month transition period, we should change the policy so that only members of the nuclear family (defined as spouses and unmarried children) of the primary immigrant would be admitted on a preferential basis. That change would remove 1.6 million from the immigration queue. Would this cause some dislocations and even heartbreak? Yes, but if America is to address the immigration crisis resolutely and effectively, it must be prepared to make some difficult choices. It has been our inability to come down on the side of our enlightened self-interest that has brought us to the precipice of ecological and psychic disaster.

After this first-step policy change, siblings of the primary immigrant would still be able to apply for admission and eventual citizenship, but would not be admitted preferentially solely on the basis of family relationships. Siblings would have to fall within numerical objectives and show they bring to their new country an educational background and skill needed at the time. In short, admission of all but the nuclear family would depend on what's best for America.

A positive change to the discussion of immigration problems would be to remove all the platitudes about "family values" from the dialogue. Favoring immigration policy that puts America's best interests first instead of family reunification does not equate to being anti-family.

Immigration to the United States is neither a human nor a civil right. If legal, it is for the benefit of the immigrant and his family at the sufferance of all other Americans. To offset the inclusion of another congestion-causing, resource-using, pollution-producing citizen, present legal residents are entitled to benefit by the addition of someone with needed skills. Simply adding another consumer/taxpayer is not a sufficient quid pro quo. If it were, why not open our borders and take in all comers?

6

The Futility of Sponsorship

Almost from the beginning, the U.S. has had restrictions in its immigration laws to exclude those likely to become "public charges." In theory, there should be *no* public charges. By law, nearly all legal immigrants (except refugees and asylees) must have a financial sponsor who pledges in writing to repay the government if means-tested benefits are paid to the immigrant within five years of arrival. However, courts across the country have held these agreements to be unenforceable. So, during the 1960s the government quietly stopped deporting immigrants who became public charges. The law still says that legal permanent resident aliens who use public benefits during their first five years in the U.S. are subject to deportation, but the law simply isn't enforced. Only forty-one people were deported on these grounds from 1961 to 1982.

The deliberate weakening of the definition of a public charge has caused the INS to issue fuzzy and misleading regulations. To the agency, there is a difference between being a "public charge" and receiving benefits. In 1999, it set out those benefits a non-citizen might receive without concern for negative immigration consequences. Non-cash benefits like food stamps, housing assistance, nutrition programs and transportation vouchers qualified. The INS publication containing this information concluded with this obfuscation: "Since the purpose of such benefits is not for income maintenance, but rather to avoid the need for ongoing cash assistance for income maintenance, they are not subject to public charge consideration."

Perhaps the INS was hoping for accolades similar to those reported by the Internal Revenue Service that claimed its organization had been recognized as "a leader in customer service." But as humor columnist Dave Barry says, that is comparable to stating that cement is a leader among construction materials for use as a dessert topping.

Time and again, we see that our government is not enforcing its immigration laws, and that taxpayers are paying for that failure. Immigration policy-by-pressure group has become so pervasive that laws are being routinely ignored to placate powerful ethnic advocacy and business lobbies. Pro-immigration interest groups have shaped both our immigration laws and their enforcement, and our inability to restrict immigration is caused by their overwhelming strength. Using competition, interaction, and bargaining, along with large doses of guile, these groups have successfully captured the initiative in shaping immigration policy. While competition and bargaining virtually define the democratic process, when they are aided and abetted by flouting the law, the system is being gamed and America is the loser.

Since our so-called sponsorship laws are widely ignored, elderly immigrants can come to the U.S. to retire in comparative luxury. The *Wall Street Journal* pointed out that in 1994 nearly 780,000 non-citizens were receiving aid from the Supplemental Security Income (SSI) program, a 580% increase — up from 127,900 in 1982 — in just twelve years. The overwhelming majority of noncitizen SSI recipients are elderly and apply for welfare within five years of arriving in the U.S. Norman Matloff of the University of California at Davis states in the *Wall Street Journal* piece that 45 percent of elderly immigrants in California received cash welfare in 1990. Based on current trends, Matloff says, the U.S. will have more than three million non-citizens and recently naturalized elderly immigrants on SSI by 2004.

Most immigrants are aware of U.S. welfare policies before they arrive. According to the *Wall Street Journal*, besides word of mouth, they receive formal counseling or read publications on how to obtain U.S. welfare benefits before leaving their home countries. For example, *What You Need to Know About Life in America* is a widely read Chinese-language publication sold in Taiwan and Hong Kong and in Chinese bookstores in the U.S. It includes a 36-page guide to SSI and other welfare benefits. *World Journal*, the U.S.'s largest circulation Chinese-language newspaper, ran a regular "Dear

The Futility of Sponsorship

Abby"-style advice column until recently on SSI and other matters of specific interest to immigrants, allowing the benefits word to be passed along.

In 1996, Congress made an effort to strengthen the INS's hand in enforcing sponsorship laws by altering a previous written agreement between the INS and the sponsor into a binding contract. Theoretically, this contract — providing for sponsors to take financial responsibility for means-tested public assistance received by immigrant relatives — is now enforceable, but based on past performance between INS and sponsors, taxpayers are entitled to be highly skeptical.

Immigration law administered overseas is equally haphazard. A U.S. consular officer stationed in the sending country first screens potential immigrants to determine, among other things, their likelihood of becoming a public charge. Since the officer works for our State Department's Consular Corps, it would be difficult to imagine two more conflicting roles than those of diplomat and an apparatchik who must inform a would-be immigrant that he or his sponsor is too poor to qualify. Also, effective screening of legal immigrant sponsors for financial solvency is not the State Department's role. Thus, the INS is the obvious choice to enforce immigration law, whether at home or abroad.

Once the immigrant is here, a fair and creative solution to the problem of enforceability of sponsorship is available. Government should require that, for the *first ten years* of an immigrant's stay in the U.S., sponsors

post a bond guaranteeing repayment to any governmental agency paying benefits to their sponsored immigrant. Sponsors would be responsible for the premium
for the bond, which would likely be $300 to $500 per
year. This might require the sponsor to pledge assets to
secure the bonding company against loss. Bonding
would place the financial responsibility for the immigrant where it belongs, squarely on the shoulders of the
immigrant and his sponsor, not on the taxpayers.

Some would ask: "Why the bond?" Experience has
shown us that the ebb and flow of public opinion
regarding immigration causes enforcement to be the
first casualty of pro-immigration pressure. Performance
bonds are enforced by the bonding company, not
bureaucrats. Posting a bond would also test the sponsor's certainty and sincerity that the immigrant will be a
self-sustaining, contributing member of our society for
at least her first ten years here.

The lack of enforcement and practical, hardheaded
provisions in our immigration policy result from the
nation's guilty conscience. Our racist past, a refusal to
shed our outdated self-perception as a "nation of immigrants," and our obsession to be perceived as a generous, hospitable people, open to the world, combine to
deny us the determination to pursue practical immigration policy. Casper Milquetoast could well be the
patron saint of those who guide enforcement policy.
Most of the necessary laws are on the books, but we

mince around ineffectively as though enforcement will offend too many segments of the population.

Ambivalence about immigration policy enforcement abounds. For instance, a provision in the 1986 Immigration Reform and Control Act (IRCA) provides for sanctions against employers hiring illegal immigrants. After the initial flurry of publicity, the government looked the other way, and employers went back to business as usual. Fifteen years after the passage of IRCA, we are doing less, not more, about our flaccid performance in policy enforcement. An employer can accept any one of 29 documents as authorization to work legally, all widely, easily, and profitably counterfeited. The other reason from no less an authority than Doris Meissner, head of the INS during the Clinton administration, is that the 291 enforcement investigators Congress is willing to fund are far too few to do the job.

Michael Huspek, an associate professor from borderclose California State University at San Marcos, made this observation in 1998:

> Migrants break the law when they enter the country without a visa; U.S. employers do too when they hire them. Yet, neither are prosecuted. "As a matter of policy, the U.S. attorney's office does not prosecute economic migrants," says Alan D. Bersin, the outgoing U.S. attorney for the Southwest region.

"When economic migrants enter the United States illegally, they are returned to their country of origin."

With anywhere from 40 percent to 70 percent of California's agricultural labor force being undocumented, the INS has been similarly reluctant to prosecute U.S. employers who rely on immigrants. In those rare instances when it has, judges have shied away from imposing tough sanctions.

These recalcitrant judges need to be reminded of Voltaire's ancient wisdom: "It is good to hang an admiral from time to time, to encourage the others."

In addition, the unwillingness of various federal agencies to cooperate with one another contributes severely to lack of enforcement. The main motivation for many immigrants to come to the U.S. in the first place is to send money home to their families. So, why not require anyone sending money out of the country to prove she is a legal resident? It is no more intrusive than proving your age when buying a drink in a bar, or gaining entrance to an R-rated movie. But to make this idea work would require cooperation among the Postal Service, Western Union, and the INS. So far, each operates autonomously and seemingly on different planets.

An egregious example of federal and local non-cooperation shows itself in the cottage industry of manufacturing counterfeit Social Security cards and other documents. According to 1999 news reports of the seizure of millions of fake green cards and Illinois drivers' licenses with a street value of as much as $800 million, Chicago and Los Angeles are the twin capitals of fake IDs. Lenient sentencing laws and a lack of sustained attention from law enforcement have contributed to this incredible illegal enterprise existing in America. The illegal document industry has largely eluded punishment from any agency.

An employee of California's Employment Development Department (EDD), who spoke on condition of anonymity, reported that when workers file for unemployment compensation, clearly presenting questionable documents, EDD employees are prevented from questioning them, or otherwise checking on the validity of their documents, because "It's not their job." Checking dubious documents constitutes discrimination. Yet, the simple act of running an electronic match of name and Social Security number could stop huge amounts of fraud.

Manuel Cunha, president of Fresno's Nisei Farmers League, was shocked by an instance of governmental non-cooperation that he encountered in 1999 while visiting Washington, D.C. In a meeting with Republican Congressman Bob Smith of Oregon, Chairman of the House Agriculture Committee, Cunha was told that, largely because of payroll deductions from *illegal immigrants,* the Social Security Administration was the recipient of a $260 billion windfall. It consists of money withheld from employees and credited to phony account numbers, printed on counterfeit Social Security cards. The contributions made by the illegal immigrant will continue to accrue to the account number each time he uses the fraudulent number to get a job, and when payroll deductions are made — a practice that can continue for decades. Not until the rightful owner of the account number actually files for Social Security benefits will the fraud sometimes be discovered. Then the Social Security Administration has to unscramble the egg, but probably gets to keep the yolk.

Our country is arguably the world leader in computerization, so why isn't the name and Social Security Number mismatch immediately discovered electronically and reported to both the employer and the INS? The result could be prompt investigation and probable deportation. The answer to why this particular enforcement activity does not exist in the Social Security Administration probably lies somewhere between "It's not my job" and partisanship.

7

Asylum and Amnesty

The constant occurrence of catastrophes, atrocities, and injustices around the world often inspire illegal emigration to the U.S., and less often lead to pleas for, and the granting of, refugee or asylum status. The INS estimates that 250,000 to 300,000 illegals enter this country each year. Of these, 100,000 successfully claim refugee status and fewer than 5,000 become successful asylum seekers.

Political asylees and refugees are essentially the same. The only difference is that those who receive asylum (asylees) do so in our country, usually at a port of entry, while refugee status is conferred in the refugee's country of origin. In both cases, the individual can apply for permanent status after one year's continuous residence in the U.S. Refugees and asylees are immediately eligible for welfare and most other social programs available to U.S. citizens, making qualification in either category extremely valuable.

Fleeing her home in Ghana for fear of genital mutilation, Adelaide Abankwah headed for the United States. Months of uncertainty here were ended when she was granted political asylum in August 1999 by the

Board of Immigration Appeals. She based her appeal on her fear of being subjected to genital cutting if she returned to Ghana. Had that occurred, she would have been one of a staggering 137 million women in at least twenty-eight African countries who have been subjected to this barbaric practice.

Paramilitary forces and narcotraffickers in Colombia are blamed for "a large share" of atrocities, including kidnapping for ransom and homicide, besetting that troubled country, according to Yves Colon, a *Miami Herald* columnist. He wrote in November 1998 that these events were causing an exodus, with many Colombians fleeing to the United States planning to apply for asylum. Juan Carlos Zapata, president of the Colombian American Service Association, feels that such dangers are sufficient to meet the U.S. requirement of "a credible fear of persecution" in order to be granted political asylum. Zapata estimated that in South Florida alone there were 40,000 Colombian expatriates.

Also in South Florida, our preferential policy toward Cubans allows any Castro protestor who can reach our shores to enter and be automatically granted political asylum. In scenes worthy of a Marx Brothers farce, members of the U.S. Coast Guard can often be found wrestling with Cubans just off shore. One combatant wants to flee the surf and set his feet on shore where freedom lies; the other is trying to do his duty to remand the Cubans back to Cuba. This so-called "wet feet policy" is often played out in the presence of hostile Cuban-American onlookers.

In addition to legitimate requests for asylum, each year thousands of creative stories of danger and oppression fall upon the desks of admitting officers. Two examples of "creative" asylum seekers are Ren Li Leng and Bi Meng Xeng, both Chinese nationals from China's Fujian province, who were arrested separately in 1994. Xeng was arrested in Honolulu when he landed there with a false Korean passport. Leng was arrested by the U.S. Coast Guard aboard a ship off Puerto Rico bound for the U.S. Both men claimed they fled China for fear they would be persecuted for violating China's one-child policy. Leng, with two boys, already had violated the policy. Xeng, 31, with one child, was apparently betting on future fecundity. He lost, because after he left, his wife filed for divorce in Switzerland. An ancient, anonymous aphorism holds that a man who claims he is boss in his own home will probably lie about other things too.

Neither Leng nor Zeng's story held water. Yet, for nearly four years their cases and appeals wound their glacial paths through our court system, while U.S. taxpayers footed the bill for their incarceration to the tune of an estimated $170,000. A much more humane and fiscally wise solution would have been to jail them for a reasonable period for having broken our immigration laws, and then to have returned them immediately to China.

In another creative asylum case, a group of scientists assembled by the INS unmasked Iftikhar Khan Chaudhry, a Pakistani seeking asylum in the U.S. by pretending to be a defector from his country's nuclear weapons program. With America's nerves frayed by frightening stories of India and Pakistan trading nuclear threats, Chaudhry held a series of news conferences here in which he claimed to have participated in a high-level military meeting in Pakistan during which a preemptive nuclear strike against India was discussed. He claimed he was ready to divulge sensitive secrets in exchange for asylum in America. When the interrogating scientists got into specifics, it became clear Chaudhry didn't know physics or nuclear weapons from curry. Subsequent questioning of officials in Pakistan revealed he was a low-paid accountant for a bathroom tile manufacturer.

So while there are many genuine cases that do warrant political asylum, there are also too many scam artists. Peter Brimelow tells of our refugee system's inability to differentiate between the two:

> . . . in early 1993 another immigration scandal erupted: it emerged that foreigners were getting off planes in New York's John F. Kennedy airport at an annualized rate rising rapidly through 15,000, applying for asylum and, because of a lack of detention space, *being released into the United States on a promise to present themselves at a future hearing,* which

not more than five percent ever did. (Not that it matters if they do. An unofficial INS estimate is that eight out of every ten asylum applicants end up staying in the United States quite regardless of whether or not their applications are approved.) *(Emphasis and parenthesis in the original)*

America's immigration laws providing for acceptance of refugees go back to the Displaced Persons Act of 1948, when it addressed the problem of the more than one million displaced persons in Germany, Austria, and Italy as a result of World War II. The Refugee Act of 1980 greatly expanded our role as a destination for the world's refugees by removing the annual numerical limitation from this category and putting the numerical limits in the hands of the president and Congress.

Current U.S. law defines a person as a refugee who is outside his country of nationality and unable or unwilling to return to that country because of "a well-founded fear of persecution." Persecution or the fear of it may be based on "an alien's race, religion, nationality, membership in a particular social group, or political opinion."

Our refugee and asylum policies were based originally on humanitarian objectives, and that focus should remain its chief purpose. Gradually, however, for lack of leadership focus and foresight regarding the long-range impact of immigration, the objectives have become more political than humanitarian. James G. Gimpel and

James R. Edwards, Jr. comment on our policy preference for refugees from communist-controlled countries:

> For example, one Cold War policy priority was to contain communist expansion. The United States therefore adopted refugee policies favorable toward those escaping communism in Cuba, Eastern Europe, and the Soviet Union. During the 1980s, as U.S. foreign policy supported the insurgent Nicaraguan Contras in their fight against the Sandinista regime, the United States admitted thousands of escaping Nicaraguan refugees.

While some Americans feel they cannot oppose those wanting to escape communism, emotion does not relate to reality — reality being the population explosion caused by immigration. As even a cursory study of current events, to say nothing of history, reveals, there will always be "emergencies" in the world. From escaping post-war Viet Nam's moribund society, to China's Tiananmen Square massacre, to the Cuban rafters escaping the foibles of Fidel's follies, there is always adequate reason to flee. Yet, so far, no consideration has been given to our own serious crises, even as we try to ameliorate them elsewhere.

In any one year, 100,000 or so refugees are not back-breaking to our population. However, when we take the longer view and add this number over a few decades, we add millions to our already crowded country. In a report released in June 2000 covering 147 countries, a leading human rights advocacy group warned that countries where people are subject to mysterious disappearance have increased by fifty-eight percent over the last decade, while torture occurs in twenty-three percent more countries than it did a decade ago.

The report pinpoints five areas "poised for tragedy." Peru and Alberto Fujimori's fallen regime is one concern. Russia's invasion of Chechnya was cited as being responsible for the flight of more than 250,000 refugees. There are fears about Zimbabwe because of the government's 1999 program to redistribute land from white commercial farmers. Indonesia, where members of the opposition party have been subject to "detention and extra judicial execution." From Xinjiang, China, come reports of Muslim minority persecution including cases of torture.

A poll reported by *The Economist* magazine in March 2000 revealed that half of those citizens interviewed in Colombia said "they would like to leave, many saying they could not live anymore with constant fear." It is estimated that some 350,000 left last year, about one percent of the population. A high proportion of the émigrés are "educated professionals, whom the country can ill afford to lose."

Warned by a friend within the government that he was about to be arrested, Christopher Atang fled his homeland of Cameroon. His crime? He was perceived by the government to be a leader in the opposition party. Some would see Atang's situation as an isolated incident; however, the United Nations High Commissioner for Refugees says he is but one of twenty-two million people forced to flee their countries in recent years. In a December 1998 report in the *Houston Chronicle,* the commissioner asserted that, one in every 255 people on the planet is a refugee. The question is: How many of these desperate people are we ready to welcome?

These 1998 and 1999 accounts from disparate countries are proxies for scores of other countries around the world whose people live day to day in harm's way. Their vulnerability is increased by cultural backwardness, less reverence for the rule of law, and danger from natural disasters exacerbated by lack of resources and infrastructure. The wealth of the U.S. combined with sympathetic immigration laws make us the world's receptive rich uncle when things get tough at home.

We can deplore and work toward the cessation of human rights violations around the world. But how far should we take our humanitarian impulses when any one of our planet's potential trouble spots could produce unpredictable numbers of refugees heading for America? And the above is only today's menu. Neither the practice of infanticide of female babies nor caste-related violence, endemic in India where seventeen percent of the world's population lives, is mentioned. The only certainty is that there will be more. Many more. Forever.

The grim reality is that we can neither provide safe haven from all the world's problems, nor right all the world's wrongs. Condoleezza Rice, George W. Bush's foreign policy advisor, declared at the Republican convention in August 2000, "We are not the world's 911."

Let's be more judicious in our admission of refugees. When unexpected disasters occur, and there is widespread public demand for raising the limits of admission for one group or another, the issue should be thoroughly and openly debated in Congress. Whatever action Congress takes should require a recorded vote so constituencies are informed of their legislators' votes. The bottom line is that refugee quota setting should be subject to considerable sunshine for the American public. It should be taken out of the politician's hands and discussed openly in front of the people.

Amnesty for illegal immigrants, a process that legalizes their status, is entirely separate from refugee and asylum issues. Legitimate seekers of refugee and asylum status are trying to play by the rules of our law. Those who are here illegally, simply waiting for the next amnesty, flout the rule of law. Yet, we repeatedly and thoughtlessly extend amnesty to these illegal immigrants.

The first provision for amnesty to illegal aliens came with the 1962 passage of legislation providing for the legalization of certain aliens who had been in the country illegally for seven to ten years. Four years later the law was expanded to include some Cuban exiles. Amnesty's big hit came in the 1986 Immigration Reform and Control Act (IRCA) legislation which forgave the illegal status of millions.

A further expansion of amnesty for illegal aliens occurred in 1997 when Congress passed the Nicaraguan Adjustment and Central American Relief Act (NACARA). This act assured "hardship" status to 250,000 Salvadorans and Guatemalans who were long-term illegal residents of the U.S., as well as certain illegal aliens from the former Soviet Union. Conferring hardship status is immigration law's way of agreeing that extreme hardship, perhaps torture or death, could result if an illegal alien is forced to return to her originating country. This makes the case for legalization much stronger. Furthermore, NACARA provided for legalization of 155,000 Nicaraguans and Cubans without having to make any hardship showing.

Amnesty for illegals in this country should be renamed "acquiescence." Just think of the chaos that would ensue if we suddenly simply acquiesced to the crimes of breaking and entering, shoplifting, burglary, and trespassing on the humanitarian grounds that the perpetrators would not have committed the illegal acts unless they were in dire need. This, in effect, is what we have done with illegal immigration by invoking amnesty.

Amnesty for illegals, which supporters claim is an act of compassion and fairness, is the most unfair way imaginable to treat the millions of law-abiding immigrants who wait their turn and abide by the rule of U.S.

law. The INS backlog of legitimate immigration requests stood at 890,000 and growing in late 1999. In addition to slowing or stopping the process of legalizing those who are patiently waiting, amnesty for illegals shouts loud and clear that we do not enforce our immigration laws against those who have already ignored them. Amnesty literally rewards those who break the law.

In addition, amnesty actually invites further illegal immigration. It sends the message to potential illegal immigrants everywhere that America is not really serious about keeping you out, so come on in, keep a low profile for a few years, and another amnesty will soon appear on the horizon.

The argument that illegal aliens should be granted amnesty because they are already here reminds one of Abraham Lincoln's debate rejoinder, "That argument is as thin as soup made by boiling the shadow of a pigeon that had been starved to death."

Because it is antithetical to the rule of law, the motives of those who promote amnesty are unavoidably suspect. The *New York Times* has editorialized about big labor's attitude toward illegals. In March 2000, it said that the AFL-CIO once saw illegals as "an economic fifth-column," which took away union jobs and depressed wages, but that the union had recently done an about-face and called for a general amnesty for illegal workers. In economic boom times with unemployment at four percent, millions of illegal aliens are seen as potential union members. Said John Wilhelm, president of the Hotel Employees and Restaurant Employees Union, "We, the labor movement, want to show we're on their side."

If that reasoning sounds somewhat politically inspired, it's not alone in the amnesty arena. Amnesty is very much about politics and the balance of power shift being sought and wrought by immigrationists.

One of the more blatantly political motives of amnesty is to swell the ranks of those likely to vote Democrat, once they are naturalized. In 1997, a typical recent year, Hispanics comprised thirty-one percent of legal immigrants. Moreover, due to our proximity to Mexico, Central America, and South America, seventy-one percent of illegal immigrants were Hispanic. In the two presidential elections prior to 2000, the Hispanic vote was overwhelmingly Democratic with seventy-two percent going to Clinton and sixty-nine percent to Dukakis.

A January 2000 *New York Times* article focused on the mathematical realities of growing Hispanic political clout. It said that by 2050 Hispanics will account for twenty-five percent of the population. The article continued, "States with the largest Hispanic populations — California, Texas, New York, and Florida — currently account for 144 of the 270 electoral votes needed to win the White House."

One of these key states, California, is home to Frank del Olmo, the widely-read oracle of the Los Angeles Latino community, and an associate editor of the *Los Angeles Times*. Mr. del Olmo has written about the deep concern of Latinos to stop the Simpson-Mazzoli bill in 1984, during the Democratic convention. Simpson-Mazzoli was a proposed, immigration-reform bill considered anti-immigrant by pro-immigration forces. Latinos fiercely opposed the bill's sanctions against employers for hiring illegals, but it was on the verge of final approval by Congress. Walter F. Mondale was widely expected to be nominated on the first ballot that year, but former U.S. Representative Edward Roybal of Los Angeles led the floor fight where many of the 340 Latino delegates threatened to embarrass Mondale by abstaining on the first ballot as a protest against Simpson-Mazzoli.

Del Olmo recalled that "The threat worked." Former House Speaker Jim Wright and other top Democrats had to strike a deal with Roybal. Simpson-Mazzoli was dead. Two years later, as a result of all the 1984 convention maneuvering, a bill much more amenable to Latinos — IRCA, with its generous general amnesty in exchange for employer sanctions — was passed.

This example of growing Latino political sophistication and clout happened seventeen years ago. Latino political power is even greater today, particularly in border states with large concentrations of Latinos. Fueled in part by repeated general amnesties, Latino political power can only grow, enhancing its ability to further its political agenda.

Columnist George F. Will has declared that this is an age when one can't find common sense without a search warrant. Congress has proved his point with repeated amnesties for illegal aliens. It started with IRCA in 1986, limited amnesty for Soviet and Indochinese nationals in 1989, and was followed by amnesty for aliens "of designated countries subject to armed conflict or natural disasters," in the Immigration Act of 1990. Their most recent folly was the Nicaraguan and Central American Relief Act of 1997 that legalized 400,000 Central American illegals. These acts, and similar legislation still being discussed, weaken the credibility of immigration law in the United States.

8

Open Borders?
They're Porous Already

> The quickest and surest way to destroy the
> American nation is to treat it as something
> other than the nation it is, just as the
> most effective way to wreck what remains of
> global order is to treat the system of integral
> nation-states as something else than what *it*
> is. If I own a horse, that horse will not sur-
> vive long if, under the delusion it is a uni-
> corn, I insist on giving it stardust to eat and
> moonbeams to drink.
> — *Chilton Williamson, Jr.*

As a tradition, every fourth of July since 1984, the *Wall
Street Journal* has run an editorial calling for a five-word
Constitutional amendment: "There shall be open borders." In the July 3, 2000 edition, editor Robert L.
Bartley rationalized his newspaper's editorial policy
with this disclaimer: "Our amendment is meant as an
ideal, to be sure, rather than an immediate policy

prescription." That so respected a newspaper as the *Wall Street Journal* would repeatedly insist on such folly and then salt the wound by calling it "an ideal" taxes the thinking reader's patience.

The ironic juxtaposition of Mr. Bartley's editorial with the two lead stories on the front page of the August 30, 2000 edition of his newspaper is almost laughable. Under the headline, "As Violence Worsens, Business Leaders Flee Colombia, Venezuela," the article details the mass exodus from these two troubled countries to Miami. Addressing the Colombian situation, the article says of Miami:

> All over this city there are signs of a large-scale exodus from the Andes, threatening new instability for a region already grappling with political and economic unrest. Tens of thousands of middle- and upper-class Colombians are fleeing to the U.S., and also Canada, Costa Rica, Spain, and Australia . . .
>
> The Colombian government estimates that 800,000 people have left during the past four years. Last year, about 366,000 applied for non-immigrant U.S. visas, more than double the number that applied in 1997. . . .

The article continues with what is happening simultaneously in Venezuela:

> Flight from Colombia comes amid a wave of emigration from its neighbor Venezuela,

spurred by President Hugo Chavez's heated rhetoric of class warfare and his erratic economic policies. . . .

Mr. Chavez was the first head of state since the Persian Gulf War to meet with Iraq's Saddam Hussein. Mr. Chavez, an admirer of Cuban leader Fidel Castro, says that both Cuba and Venezuela are flowing toward the same "sea of happiness."

Powered by this instability, a wave of violent robberies and kidnappings is also driving people out of Venezuela, which further emphasizes the folly of open borders championed by the editorial opinion of the *Wall Street Journal.* The right-hand story on the front page of the same August 30, 2000 *Wall Street Journal* is entitled: "As Economy Hums, Congested Freeways Exact a Heavy Toll." It begins with a vignette about a bureaucrat's commute into Washington, D.C.:

On his hourlong commute to the nation's capital from his home twenty-four miles away . . . it often takes Mr. Demidenko, a medical librarian at the Library of Congress, thirty minutes to negotiate a two mile stretch where Interstate 270 funnels into the Capital Beltway. Sometimes the interchange is so jammed with vehicles that he can't make it across four lanes of traffic in time, and he overshoots his exit.

The scene then shifts to California's storied Silicon Valley to discuss the deterioration of local commuting:

> Twenty-six miles of bumper-to-bumper traffic on Route 101 have turned what ten years ago was a thirty minute commute between San Mateo, Calif., and San Jose into a seventy-five minute drive. . . .
>
> The average delay per driver per year in the sixty-eight largest U.S. cities has risen to fifty hours from thirty-four hours a decade ago, according to the Texas Transportation Institute. And there's no relief in sight. . . .
>
> Paul Dempsey, a transportation professor at the University of Denver, says that eliminating such snarls could save more than $100 billion a year — and do for transportation what the Internet has done for communications.

Neither of these well-researched articles, one about the flight from unstable situations in South America to the U.S. and the other concerning our hugely overcrowded transportation corridors, makes a causal connection with immigration policy. The careful reader, however, will read between the lines.

Eager to impress his countrymen with "creative" ideas, the charismatic new president of Mexico, Vincente Fox, has also proposed open borders between his country and the U.S. Since the World Bank estimates that as many as forty percent of Mexico's 100 million people have incomes of less than $2 per day, perhaps President Fox can be forgiven his brief dalliance with stardust and moonbeams. But with such an income disparity compared to the U.S., the flood of Mexican economic immigrants who would cross an open border risks overwhelming the border states and the rest of the U.S.

To refute President Fox's proposal of open borders, George Borjas, Harvard professor and prolific author on the subject of immigration, says this:

> Puerto Ricans are American citizens who can move freely within the United States, and the differences in economic opportunities between Puerto Rico and the mainland are quite large. Not surprisingly, about twenty-five percent of Puerto Rico's population moved to the United States in the last fifty years. Even if the Mexican migration response were only half that of Puerto Rico, total Mexican immigration to the United States could conceivably be 12.5 million, compared with the current 7 million.

Our porous borders already allow a waterfall of illegals and their children to cascade upon a nation beset with the problems of *legal* immigration. Not only does our government pretend that illegals are not breaking the law, it continues to educate their children. The illegals know this paradox exists and take advantage of it.

The simultaneous states of illegal immigrant and legal student are inconsistent and irrational. About forty percent of our illegal aliens gain access to the U.S. by obtaining tourist or other temporary visas, flying to any U.S. port of entry as visitors, then disappearing. If apprehended, which is rare, they go back home to try again. By the INS's own estimate, visa overstayers swell our population by 110,000 people annually. The other sixty percent of the estimated 275,000 illegal immigrants each year penetrate our borders by various creative schemes.

Border games are common in the San Diego district of the Border Patrol, a division of the INS. Several Spanish language signs in the headquarters, where all apprehended illegal border crossers are detained for booking, set the atmosphere. These signs advise all detainees of a toll-free 800 number and convenient telephones they can use, courtesy of U.S. taxpayers, to report any displeasure they may have about their apprehension or subsequent treatment. A snack of juice and raisins is provided for all who are apprehended.

Adding a note of seriousness to the border game, all detainees are booked utilizing a new computerized system. By placing their fingers on an electronic pad, they allow the computer to store their fingerprints and simultaneously photograph them. Their mug shots and fingerprints immediately become part of the nationwide INS database. Should they be subsequently apprehended in San Diego or any other INS location, their pictures and records of all prior INS arrests will be automatically displayed, triggered by the computer recognizing their fingerprints.

Border patrol agents say that when the system was first installed in the late 1990s, it took twenty-nine prior arrests to result in prosecution. By 2000, that number in San Diego was substantially reduced, but depended on the workload of the local U.S. Attorney's office rather than the severity of the offense.

Booking is followed by a videotaped presentation. It contains warnings about the severe weather hazards to migrants in eastern San Diego County, a route increasingly favored by illegals as the border around San Diego becomes more difficult to cross. Also emphasized are the dangers of dealing with smugglers, or, in the parlance of the border, "coyotes," who frequently rob, rape, or otherwise abuse the illegal immigrants they purport to serve. The tape is in Spanish, and a featured spokesman is the reassuring local Mexican Consul General. The attitude and atmosphere are permeated by friendliness and respect, as if the lawbreakers were guests in our home. One almost forgets that the people being dealt with here have just been apprehended while committing a crime.

What happens next is equally contradictory. All detainees are offered their choice of either voluntary return (VR) or a formal judicial hearing. Over ninety-five percent opt for VR, which amounts to a free bus ride back across the border to nearby Tijuana. If someone opting for VR is from deep in Mexico, say Mexico

City, and has no money, the U.S. taxpayers provide an airline ticket for his return flight. He is warned that should he be rearrested for illegal entry within five years, he will be prosecuted.

The entire proceeding is almost whimsical. The coyotes have a name for it: *"Es un juego,"* — "It's a game."

The game is so easily played that immigrant smuggling has become a growth industry. In Texas, a University of Houston study published in December 1998, and reported by the *San Antonio Express News* revealed that more than 1,600 deaths, most undocumented immigrants who drowned or dehydrated while trying to sneak into this country, were recorded along the border in a five-year period that ended in 1997. The *Express News* said that most of the deaths were from drowning, heat, or other environmentally related causes, and homicide.

Many of these deaths result from unscrupulous smugglers leading illegal immigrants through hazardous terrain to avoid beefed-up border enforcement at customary crossing points. If the going gets tough, the coyotes often abandon the illegals, some of whom subsequently die.

During October 1998, in Miami, Florida, every state and federal law enforcement agency in South Florida met to discuss the problem of organized smuggling of illegal aliens. B. G. Kring, chief of the Border Patrol sector in Florida, contends that these days his people face smugglers equipped with fast boats and global position-ing devices instead of the rafters and slow wooden boats of old. "What's changed is the sophistication of the smugglers is picking up and the money is bigger. Fees range from $1,000 for a hop from the Bahamas to $45,000 for people smuggled in from Asia."

By the spring of 2000, smuggling fees in San Diego were also on the rise. Fees that once were $50 to $100 to cross the Mexican border became $500 to $1500. Equally significant, in 1999 in San Diego, people from fifty-three different countries were arrested as they attempted to enter the United States illegally.

There are also too many ways to beat the patrol sys-tem. Seven miles from the Mexican border, Richard Gaona operates from a tiny two-room office tucked behind Rosario's Hair Studio in McAllen, Texas. His business is supplying U.S. meatpackers, poultry plants, and farms with workers, mostly from Mexico. Gaona is paid about $300 per worker for the 300 to 600 workers he supplies to his clients each year.

Gaona is one of thousands of brokers who help bring immigrants and labor-hungry employers to-gether. The problem is that a substantial, uncertain percentage of the workers he supplies are illegal immi-grants, and our laws allow him and his peers to ignore the distinction with impunity. When pressed about the immigration status of the workers he supplies, Mr. Gaona replies: "Look, of course there will be some who do not tell the truth. What can anyone do about that?"

Mr. Gaona and his peers, while an important source of illegals, are responsible for only part of the flow. According to the INS's own figures, over five million illegal immigrants reside in the U.S. today. Their number swells by more than a quarter of a million each year, and once they are inside our borders our laws make it difficult, if not impossible, to identify and deport them.

Mr. Gaona is shielded by the same Catch 22 as the illegals themselves, their employers, and their agents all over our country. Under federal law, employers are not required to determine if documents presented by a worker are authentic. In fact, if employers question the authenticity of documents simply because the candidate looks or sounds foreign, they risk charges of employment discrimination. According to a statement by IBP, a large Mid-Western meatpacker: "There is a fine line employers must walk between federal laws that protect employee rights and those that prohibit the employment of undocumented workers."

In addition, once they are here, workers can present over two dozen different documents to establish their legal employability, most of the IDs easily counterfeited and widely available. This has spawned another illegal growth industry, that of making and marketing counterfeit documents. The most popular acceptable documents, and therefore the ones most often counterfeited, are green cards, driver's licenses, birth certificates, and Social Security cards. Among others, the "Latin Kings," a Chicago street gang, have moved in on this illegal, multi-million dollar business, "branding it with violence and intimidation" according to a September 1999, *Chicago Tribune* story.

Peter Brimelow has researched the widespread use of counterfeit documents and its expense to American taxpayers. He says that eighty-three percent of illegal immigrants amnestied under IRCA had false Social Security numbers and that local agencies are now essentially forbidden by confidentiality laws from reporting fraud to the INS, according to that agency itself. Brimelow also asserts that the Internal Revenue Service makes no effort to prevent illegal aliens from receiving earned income tax credit refunds, which are sometimes payable even if no income tax is due and can exceed two thousand dollars.

An illegal Mexican immigrant, who would agree to be identified only as "Mr. Guzman" for a story in the *Washington Post*, said he bought fake green cards and Social Security numbers for $120 apiece. "If one doesn't buy these papers, one can't work," said the 53-year-old Mr. Guzman. He reports that, in addition to obtaining a job, he used his false documents to create a whole new identity. The phony IDs made possible a driver's license, credit cards, bank accounts, auto registration, the filing of tax returns, and eventually a $130,000 mortgage on a house. These multiple deceptions are possible only because there is presently no practical way for an employer or anyone else to determine if Mr. Guzman is a legal resident.

The proliferation of counterfeit ID is worsening with the growth of Internet access. All the documents mentioned above are now available on the Internet, so an illegal or someone he hires can now point and click his way to a new identity. One site advertises: "We will provide you with exact . . . replicas in every detail of the current state IDs . . . We do whatever security measure that state has (i.e. UV, watermark, hologram, seal, reflective laminate coating)."

Such bravado on the part of counterfeiters emphatically proves the need to take a hard-line approach to determining who is and is not legally employable. Since jobs are the main magnet pulling a quarter of a million illegal immigrants yearly into our already crowded country, we need — in addition to establishing a credible fear of punishment — to establish the certainty that only those with authentic proof of their legal status will be granted the privilege of working here. And the only way to do that is with a counterfeit-proof identification card that proves identity and legality. Today, that function is supposedly filled by the Social Security card, but the card is too easily counterfeited, and the government makes no real effort to identify, apprehend, and punish those who use it fraudulently. Enforcement of this and other security measures are as hit-and-miss as stopping illegals at the border. The usefulness of the Social Security card as a means of establishing identity and legality has been destroyed by the ease with which it can be counterfeited. Eighty-three percent of the millions amnestied under IRCA had fake Social Security cards.

Biometrics is a technology that could stop counterfeiting because it uses individual personal characteristics such as fingerprints, palm prints, hand geometry, voice verification, retinal scanning, iris scanning, and facial recognition. All of these approaches are in use today, sometimes individually, sometimes in combination. Earlier in this chapter, we wrote of an already up-and-running biometric system, that of the automated fingerprint and mug shot system the INS uses to identify previously apprehended illegals.

In the short time since that leading-edge system was introduced, an even better fingerprint-based approach to combating counterfeiting has emerged. The newest technology monitors electrical impulses given off by the ridges and valleys of living tissue. Its chips look past the first layer of skin — as well as any dirt — to the live layer. This breakthrough technology will bring down costs and produce a higher percentage of successful first-time reads.

A biometric Social Security card could begin with "enrollment." Just as it is today, every person wishing to work would be required to have a Social Security number, but the difference would be that she must enroll by having her biometric characteristics recorded in a chip imbedded in her "smart" Social Security card. When she applies for a job, her employer would be required to verify her eligibility to work in this country. In large organizations, this would be done through a computer terminal. Prospective employees of smaller employers would take their cards to the local Social Security or INS office for certification. A key element of this approach would be enforced sanctions against employers who fail to require presentation and certification of the card when hiring.

Of course, there are costs associated with the issuance and implementation of the smart Social Security card, and inevitably, some people will object to this program on the basis that it constitutes an invasion of privacy. In fact, it adds nothing to the loss of anonymity not already present with the existing Social Security card system. It simply assures that the person presenting the card and its associated Social Security number is the legitimate owner of that card and number.

It would seem that only the latest technology could thwart the deluge of illegal aliens. In San Diego, aggressive new programs utilizing the latest innovations have been designed to gain control of problematic sectors of the border. "Operation Gatekeeper" in San Diego, as well as "Safeguard" in Nogales, Arizona, "Hold the Line" in El Paso, Texas, and "Operation Rio Grande" in Brownsville, Texas, are all up and running. Some examples of the exotic (and expensive) equipment in these hot-spots: Atop 60-foot reinforced steel poles sit four remote-controlled, bulletproof cameras. At night they can pick up body heat images as far as one and one half miles away. Underground sensors, 10,000 of them in the San Diego sector, pick up any movement. LORIS, a long-range infrared system, is sensitive enough to locate a rabbit five miles away. Portable, it can be taken into the field by agents and mounted on a tripod at strategic locations. Fiber optic borescopes about eight inches long and two inches in diameter, similar to the cameras designed to peer inside the human body, can inspect closed areas in vehicles, searching for human cargo or, for that matter, smuggled drugs. New night vision goggles are described as a quantum leap in technology. Hand-held, battery-operated spotlights can project intense beams of light that reach up to two miles. These spotlights have infrared beams, providing agents a light source that can't be seen by the target. The capstone of all this technology is intelligent, computer-aided detection systems, which can tell agents when ground sensors are not working properly. Eventually, a national network would allow agents in Washington, D.C., to view activity across all sectors with almost no lagtime.

So far, though, the dismal result of spending hundreds of millions of taxpayers' dollars on this high-tech hardware is to force the coyotes to reroute migrants into lightly patrolled, often-dangerous entry points. The flood of undocumented immigrants continues unabated, just like Ole Man River.

The reason? The Border Patrol, for all its high-tech equipment, is totally outnumbered by the skill and cunning of the coyotes and their passengers. Disturbingly, this lack of prevention of border crossings has given birth to echoes of the old west and vigilante justice. A July 1999 lead story in *USA Today* reported the reaction to the breakdown of law and order near Douglas, Arizona:

> Seemingly overnight, little Douglas, a town of fewer than 18,000 people, finds itself in the center of it all. In March alone, 27,000 migrants were caught by the local Border Patrol station, the same as were detained here in all of 1993 . . .
>
> They litter the land with plastic water bottles. They clip fences, allowing cattle to escape. To slake their own thirst, they break the water pipes that keep ranchers' herds alive . . .
>
> One night in April, 600 people rushed the border at once, and the outnumbered Border Patrol managed to round up barely a third of them . . .
>
> Douglas Mayor Ray Borane, the bilingual son of a Mexican mother says . . . "We're being invaded . . . patience is wearing thin. I'm afraid someday there's going to be a tragedy."

Sadly, the article could be written about many other areas along the Mexican border, where illegal immigrant traffic moves and shifts. Incipient vigilantism is on the rise along the border, according to the article. The Mexican Foreign Ministry complained in 1999 that there were twenty-four instances of armed ranchers in Cochise County, Arizona, detaining groups of illegals.

As citizens become more aware of the invasion from the south, they will force our elected officials to put a stop to it. But cracking down on border security will complicate our desire to maintain the very special and envied relationship we have with Canada. A common language and each other's largest export market enhance this coveted relationship, much stronger than our relationship with Mexico. And the present contrast between the relative calm on our Canadian border and the chaos on the Mexican border could not be more stark. The INS estimates that about 150,000 illegal aliens per year enter the U.S. via the Mexican border, while the estimated annual illegal flow from Canada is 6,000 to 12,000.

Yet, when one smuggling route becomes blocked, determined smugglers simply switch to another. As was the case in the 1990s when cocaine entering the U.S. through Florida was blocked from that route, smugglers began using Mexico as their route and the flow of drugs into the U.S. continued unabated. The Canadian border is the next area of porosity in illegal immigration. More than $1 billion in goods and services cross the Canadian border daily, and there are more than 200 million individual border crossings annually. Additionally, there are an estimated 95,000 people who live in Canada and work in the U.S.

Our resolve to apply the same measures to the Canadian border we do to the Mexican border has already been weighed and found wanting. In 1996, Congress passed the Illegal Immigration Reform and Immigrant Responsibility Act, calling for the implementation of an automated INS system to document every alien entering or leaving the U.S. The purpose was to prevent visa overstaying. As the deadline for implementation in 1998 approached, pressure from both Canada and representatives of northern border states mounted. Canadian Ambassador Raymond Chretien complained: "This isn't the time to block up the border." This combined pressure from the U.S. and Canada resulted in legislation to delay implementation "while more feasible controls are studied." To date, no more has been done.

While such changes must be made thoughtfully and with due consideration of our people and our valued Canadian friends, the status quo is only a license for further invasion. We must successfully resist illegal immigration at all points on our borders, not self-deceptively reroute.

Simply stated, our illegal immigration problem is caused by the overwhelming desirability of living and working in America, and obviously, we don't want to change that. What must change is the balance of resolve. Today, the resolve of those who decide to emigrate to the U.S. illegally far exceeds ours to restrict them. Most of the time, they win.

Enabling a law calls for both effective enforcement and deterrents. How effective would speed limits or the laws against trespassing be without deterrents? Without the threat of a traffic ticket, the desire to get there a little sooner would dominate our behavior, public safety be damned. Without the threat of fines, jail, or other sanctions, our laws respecting private property would also be ignored in favor of certain selfish motives. The balance of resolve must be on society's side, and the best way to establish this balance is by broadcasting that the chances of successfully breaching our borders are remote. A corollary should be that if the illegal *is* apprehended, punishment will be certain and costly.

The only effective punishment for illegal entry is to remove the ability to work. That means incarceration. Three months for the first infraction, six months for the second, and a year for the third and each subsequent conviction, would seem to be severe enough, yet reasonable enough to achieve the desired deterrent effect. With such a radical new approach, a warning should be widely advertised around the world for six months prior to implementation. Newspapers, the electronic media, and our embassies could spread the news: "America welcomes, as it always has, productive, law abiding immigrants, but will no longer tolerate illegal immigration. If you attempt it and are caught, *you will go to jail.*"

Jailing illegal immigrants will cost us some serious money, to be sure. However, when weighed against the benefits of reducing the impact on our schools and other infrastructure, and stopping the escalating rate of population growth with its attendant diminution of our quality of life, the costs will be less over the long term. With the availability of recently, or soon to be closed, military bases around the country, the investment in bricks and mortar could be minimal. And, best of all, admittedly large initial costs will be temporary. Once the word gets around that the U.S. is really serious about solving the illegal immigration problem, their numbers at our borders should rapidly diminish. The real enforcement of incarceration can tip the balance of resolve in favor of the rule of law.

At the end of the day, the best and most lasting way to help overcrowded nations is to assist them in improving conditions at home so their citizens find prosperity and fulfillment on their own turf.

Mexico is an example of a country where it would be demonstrably more compassionate for its government to work towards making emigration unnecessary, rather than asking the U.S. to serve as safety valve for its jobless and dispossessed. Since 1981, America has admitted about four million legal Mexican immigrants and an additional three million illegals. This has done

Mexico no good; its economy is weak and getting weaker.

In an article entitled "Mexico — Let Them Eat Hamburger," the *Economist* asserted that "Thirty-six percent of workers were paid less than the minimum wage in 1997, compared with thirty percent in 1991." The magazine continued, "The minimum wage itself has been falling for over two decades — it is now just under 35 pesos ($3.55) a day — while basic supplies have gone up in price." Of course, Mexican workers caught in this economic vise have fled in droves, mostly for the United States. A December 1998, *New York Times* article reported that perhaps fifteen percent of the Mexican electorate lived north of the border. Those millions of Mexican voters would be more valuable and helpful to their country by remaining in Mexico as consumers, tax payers, voters, and activists for change. Mexico's problems will never be solved by running away from them.

9

Assimilation Is Not Working

> The one absolutely certain way of bringing
> this nation to ruin ... would be to permit
> it to become a tangle of squabbling nation-
> alities.
>
> — *President Theodore Roosevelt*

The United States has a proud tradition of assimilating immigrants, but successful assimilation is multifaceted. It must start with a desire by the immigrant to become a vital part of his new land, not merely a resident. As command of the common language improves, so does acceptance. Then come the physical manifestations of assimilation: successful employment, home ownership, and the ultimate act of assimilation, naturalization.

Today's legal immigrant does not fit the stereotype of the bearded Ellis Island immigrant of yesteryear who saved for years to afford the weeks-long steamship passage to America. Now he is whisked by jet in hours from China to Chicago, from New Delhi to New York, at a fraction of the earlier cost converted to current dollars. Gone are the days of the wrenching final farewell to home and hearth. If today's immigrant doesn't like it, or make it, in the land of opportunity, or if he needs to vacate and rejuvenate, he simply jumps on a jet to return home. This ability to easily pull up stakes does not make for long-term commitment to the host country.

Gone also is the isolation of the past. Low cost, long-distance telephone calls are commonplace. According to Sheldon Hochheiser, corporate historian for AT&T, trans-Atlantic phone calls, first possible in 1927, were prohibitively expensive — $200 in current dollars for a three-minute call to London. Over time, costs came down. Hochheiser says, "In 1965 it cost $10.59 to call the Dominican Republic for three minutes and $15 to call India; now those rates are $1.71 and $3.66 respectively."

Faxes, e-mail, and video tapes also provide bridges to the native country. The following 1998 vignette recounted in the July 19, 1998 *New York Times,* took place in New York City. It dramatically illustrates that staying in touch is only getting easier:

> Mr. Ali sat nervously before a large computer screen in the darkened conference room of Satellite Tech Telecommunication . . .
>
> Without warning, the screen came to life, and the image of his older sister, draped in a floral head scarf . . . appeared live from

Islamabad . . . and she had a thing or two on
her mind . . . At $5 a minute his sister, Shamim
Kusar, harangued him for not writing . . .
Their father thought he no longer cared for
them she reported; now he was American.
When Mr. Ali's eyes brimmed Mrs. Kusar
softened. She told her brother he looked weak
and underfed. He told her he was working
too hard, that everyone worked too hard in
America, which is why it is such a prosperous
country . . . "I will tell mother you are fat."
She reached out to tickle his face on the
screen. "I will tell everyone in town that I saw
my brother on TV,' she said, giggling. "They
won't believe me. We are simple people."
     "Pray to Allah for me, dear sister," he
answered, biting back tears . . .

Such recently available connectivity, while salving the
hurt of separation, also slows or halts the process of
assimilation. The new country provides the financial
wherewithal, but the native country is where the heart
is. And while it was not such a problem to totally assimilate just over one-half million immigrants from all over
the world during the 1930s, the approximately twelve
million legal and illegal newcomers during the 1990s
remain only partially Americanized because of their
huge numbers and changed attitudes within the U.S.
regarding assimilation.

Assimilation Is Not Working

Mexicans, while far from the only source of immigrants, dominate. There is no other instance in the world where a First World country shares so extensive a land border with a Third World country, as the U.S. does with Mexico. This 2,000-mile border, the enormous income differential, and the lack of success in protecting our border combine to make Mexicans our single largest group of immigrants, accounting for eighteen percent of legal immigrants in 1997. Four million Mexican-Americans resided legally in the U.S. as of 1996, with an estimated additional three million illegal immigrants from Mexico.

Unfortunately for our nation's cohesiveness, this largest group of immigrants has the least need for assimilation. Not only can the four million legal and three million illegal Mexican immigrants go home frequently and relatively cheaply, but also they usually live among their countrymen here and culturally dominate the areas in which they live.

The town of Highland Park, California, a suburb of Los Angeles, has become almost entirely Latino. The main street, Pacific Boulevard, could well have been pre-assembled in Mexico. Latin music blares from record shops, toy stores sell piñatas — a staple of Mexican parties — the tang of tacos, enchiladas, and refried beans permeates. Store signs and the buzz of conversation are in Spanish. In their homes, Mexican expatriates tune into a rich variety of radio and TV in their native tongue and read Spanish language newspapers and magazines. The immigrant might as well be in Mexico City or Mazatlan. Compare these amenities with those of earlier immigrants who, with the exception of the occasional small circulation native-language newspaper, had little native-country influence.

According to Alejandro Carrillo Castro, a former Mexican consul general in Chicago, Mexicans living in the U.S. are far more reluctant than other nationalities to naturalize, taking an average of twenty-two years compared with seven years for others. Max Lucatero, the once-illegal Mexican immigrant described in chapter five, has been in Southern California since 1980. He has a wife and two children, a successful small business, and professes great love for America, but although legalized by the 1986 amnesty and "working on" naturalization, he still hadn't become a citizen by the new millennium.

In 1998, Mexico passed legislation allowing dual citizenship for all Mexicans living abroad. This idea invites naturalized Mexican-American immigrants to violate their oath renouncing foreign loyalties, which is part of the naturalization procedure. It is also detrimental to the process of assimilation.

A troubling example of some Mexican immigrants' divided loyalties was reported in this May 1988 article in the *Houston Chronicle:*

> At a soccer game against Mexico in February, the American national team listened in frus-

tration as a chorus of boos erupted during
"The Star Spangled Banner."

Thousands of fans threw cups and bottles
at the United States players, often striking
them. They also attacked someone in the
stands who tried to unfurl an American flag.

The match didn't take place in Mexico
City but in Los Angeles. Most of the fans
were Mexican or Mexican-American. The
extreme reactions to their behavior were dis-
heartening but predictable.

Although thirty-one other countries, including Canada, allow dual citizenship, it is well to remember the
ancient admonition that blood is thicker than water. It
is reasonable and prudent to ask where the loyalties of
the expatriates from those thirty-one countries would
lie should the U.S. come into conflict, armed or otherwise, with their native land. No one minimizes the sac-
rifices of the tens of thousands of immigrants from
many countries who have fought and died for the U.S.
However, this movement toward multiple citizenship is
unwise and should end. U.S. citizenship laws should be
zealously enforced. It is time for both the U.S. and its
immigrants to again take seriously the oath to renounce
all foreign loyalties.

When we forget the lessons of history, which show
assimilation as so essential to successful immigration,
we invite serious and disruptive problems. One such

problem is in the legal sphere. Our legal system should demand, as a vital element of assimilation, that an immigrant seeking legal status as a permanent U.S. resident, obey our laws even though they may conflict with the cultural morés of his native country.

Many dramatic recent examples of cultural morés, foreign to our customs, contrary to our laws, have been observed on our soil. Earlier, we discussed the widespread practice of female genital cutting, which is illegal in the U.S. Adherents argue that one person's genital cutting is another's circumcision. According to a *New York Times* article this conflict had a Seattle hospital attempting to invent a harmless female circumcision procedure, less brutal than the traditional versions, but satisfactory to conservative Somali immigrant parents wanting to maintain this African custom. "The idea got buried in criticism from an outraged public."

Matters of family honor are addressed savagely in some countries. There are several countries in the Middle East where a wronged family may demand the death penalty and carry it out themselves with official blessing. When such practices take place on U.S. soil in defiance of U.S. law, most Americans are outraged. To prevent such aberrations, the INS needs to carefully research foreign customs, by country, and identify those that are clearly contradictory to our legal system. The agency could then provide educational information for immigrants, prior to their admission, explaining that certain practices, acceptable in their home country, are illegal here. If would-be immigrants find our cultural morés unacceptable, they have the option of searching out a country more sympathetic to their customs.

Los Angeles and Miami are metaphors for the affliction of poor assimilation. In Los Angeles, huge enclaves of Mexicans dominate; in Miami, Cubans. Both communities are Spanish-speaking and include people from many other Central and South American countries. In essence, they constitute countries within a country. One Los Angeles Latino leader explained that assimilation was less an imperative with his people than with earlier immigrant waves. He asserted that today's Mexican immigrants are able to maintain their "Mexicanness" due to the prevalence of Spanish language radio and television (much of it beamed from stations in nearby Mexico), plus Spanish-language advertising and printed media, and bi-lingual education. The same comparison pertains to the "Cubanos" and other Latinos in Miami. This is bad news for the process of assimilation.

Floridians agreed with this assessment in the mid-1990s. Seventy-seven percent of non-Hispanic Whites and seventy-two percent of non-Hispanic Blacks thought the quality of life in Florida had been diminished by Cuban immigration. A mere one percent thought it had been improved. This is a complaint about the sheer magnitude of the immigration, not about the immigrants themselves. Huge numbers defy assimilation, and lack of assimilation spells friction.

In July 2000, contributing editor Robert J. Samuelson of *Newsweek* magazine wrote about the threat of balkanization inherent in such concentrations:

> The power of America's economy, culture, and society to assimilate immigrants is enormous . . . But that power is not unlimited. The job market, schools and social services can be overwhelmed by large numbers . . . The dangers are balkanization — a society increasingly fractured along class and ethnic lines — and a backlash against immigration.

Half-hearted immigration enforcement, such as America suffers today, leads to these large concentrations, especially near our borders and coastlines. Not only our largest cities but those situated near the Mexican border such as El Paso, San Antonio, and San Diego, and those on our vulnerable coastline, like San Francisco, Fort Lauderdale, and Orlando must cope with unassimilated concentrations of immigrants.

The Fourteenth Amendment to the U.S. Constitution was passed in 1868 for the express purpose of insuring full citizenship rights to freed slaves. It states in part: "All persons born or naturalized in the United States, and subject to the jurisdiction thereof, are citizens of the United States and of the state wherein they reside." A tortured misinterpretation of this single sentence holds that any child born on U.S. soil, regardless of its mother's immigration status, is a U.S. citizen. As recently as 1996, in California alone, 100,000 children of illegal aliens became automatic U.S. citizens. Three-quarters and two-thirds respectively of babies born in the county hospitals of San Diego and Los Angeles that year were born to illegal alien mothers, generally from Mexico.

When a child becomes a U.S. citizen, the illegal immigrant parents are much more difficult to deport. Illegal parents can claim most of the welfare benefits designed to help legitimate low-income American families. After all, their child *is* an American citizen. As soon as the child reaches eighteen, he or she can sponsor parents and siblings for legal status under our chain immigration laws, and those parents and siblings can sponsor theirs. It would be difficult to conjure up a less logical interpretation of the Fourteenth Amendment than this border-busting bit of altruism.

Most of the industrialized world takes a much more common-sense view of birthright citizenship. In Japan, France, Germany, and Russia, a newborn's citizenship depends on that of the parents. And while England had a policy such as ours until 1983, it now requires that at least one parent of a new baby be a legal resident for that baby to be a citizen. Australia has a similar requirement. And the folly of our present policy has not entirely escaped our Congress, either. The 104th Congress (January 1995–January 1997) did consider six separate bills on the subject. Unfortunately, it passed none.

The failure of these bills to become law suggests not only a lack of Congressional will, but also makes quite clear that it will be a very long time, or never, before the Congress of the United States passes birthright citizenship legislation. However, the Twenty-first Amendment to the U.S. Constitution, the amendment to repeal prohibition, took only a year to pass, after the legislatures of two-thirds of the states called forty-eight constitutional conventions, as provided for in Article V of the Constitution. It is thus theoretically possible that if public opinion becomes sufficiently inflamed over an issue, citizens can appeal for action without the need for Congressional legislation.

The abuse of the Fourteenth Amendment, as stated earlier in this chapter, is but one example of the "dumbing down" of the process of gaining citizenship. Naturalization has been pushed to the brink of irrelevancy by misinterpretation and lack of enforcement of our own laws. Immigrants can apply for citizenship here after five years of legal residence and passing an FBI background check to insure they have no criminal records. The law requires an INS interviewer to determine that they can speak, read, and write simple English and answer correctly seven out of twelve random questions about American history and government.

But even this modest set of requirements is not met. The investigation of David P. Schippers, former Chief Counsel for the House Judiciary Committee uncovered many abuses surrounding Vice President Al Gore's all-out effort to naturalize and register hundreds of thousands of immigrants in time to vote in the 1996 presidential election. The program was labeled "Citizenship USA" (CUSA), and according to Mr. Schippers, Vice President Gore "was responsible for keeping the pressure on [the INS] to make sure the aliens were pushed through by September 1, the last day to register for the presidential election." Schippers reports that the pressure manifested itself in several ways:

> INS agents in district offices were directed to relax the testing for English, complete every interview within twenty minutes, and ensure that all applicants pass the civics test by continuing to ask questions until an applicant got a sufficient number right . . . The White House, the INS, and the Justice Department publicly denied any political motive in the CUSA program to expedite the citizenship procedure. What the United States got is undeniable:
>
> 1. More than 75,000 new citizens who had arrest records when they applied;
> 2. An additional 115,000 citizens whose fingerprints were unclassifiable for various technical reasons and were never resubmitted; and

3. Another 61,000 people who were given citizenship with no fingerprints submitted at all.

Those numbers were developed by the accounting firm of KPMG Peat Marwick as a result of an audit of the 1996 CUSA program.

Elaine Koomis, an INS spokeswoman, reported in 1999 that the increasing number of would-be citizens was so great that the backlog of naturalization applications had grown to 1.8 million. According to Koomis: "Before 1996, the system was set up to handle 300,000 applications a year. This year [1999] the agency has received 770,000 applications and expects to get another 700,000 in 2000." Absent a fundamental change in national priorities, budget constraints and these staggering numbers combine to insure the continued decline of naturalization standards for the foreseeable future.

Perhaps the most serious indictment of U.S. assimilation efforts are growing signs that English is wavering as our national language. "The INS has already conducted a swearing-in service almost entirely in Spanish and is testing a program to conduct citizenship exams [entirely] in foreign languages."

The proliferation of states allowing drivers' tests in foreign languages, ATMs in banks and stores offering cash in several languages, cities and counties printing ballots in multiple languages, public utilities doing likewise when printing their regulations, only help to trap immigrants in the quicksand of linguistic inadequacy. Contrary to the multi-culturalist's psychobabble about self-esteem diminished through assimilation, *learning English* is *the single most important thing immigrants can do* to help them succeed in our English-speaking society. A famous outsider, France's Alexis de Tocqueville, observed, "The tie of language is perhaps the strongest and most durable that can unite mankind."

An immigrant's mastery of the native language, whether German, French, Arabic, or English, is a condition-precedent to assimilation in any country. And, assimilation is a win-win proposition; the immigrant wins because he has a better chance of competing successfully, and the new homeland wins because it has another productive, educable and, therefore, informed citizen. This is a fact, not speculation. U.S. Labor Department statistics show that English-speaking immigrants earn over three times as much as those wedded to a foreign language. A mid-1990's study of Vietnamese and Laotian refugees found the following differences in hourly wages: "No English: $4.35 an hour; basic words $5.16; short conversation: $6.30; five- to ten-minute conversation: $8.45; fluent, $14.82 an hour."

In spite of these statistics, in many jurisdictions, if a protected minority constitutes five percent or more of a voting district, both ballots and voter information pamphlets must be printed multilingually. In Los Angeles County sample ballots are printed in English, Chinese,

Tagalog (Filipino), Japanese, Vietnamese, and Spanish. As of 1999, 375 voting districts throughout the U.S. were printing ballots in foreign languages.

Canadian attempts at multiculturalism are an example of disaster writ large. The late Canadian Prime Minister, Pierre Trudeau, advocated a policy that opponents say has promoted intolerance by immigrants for Canadian culture and institutions. The French language, rather than religion or culture, was the cause of Quebec's secessionist movement, causing the Parti Quebecois government to place restrictions on English schools in the province. Languages other than French are banned in most places. If the U.S. continues down the road of weakening English as its common language, it is probable that a language-based separatist movement will develop in parts of the United States.

Bilingual education, masquerading as a friend of immigrants, is actually an archenemy and is ardently counterproductive. It lulls those involved into a sense of progress, while diminishing the urgency of their assimilation into the mainstream of America. The concept of bilingual education began with the Cuban refugees in Florida. Most Floridians, and Cubans themselves, saw refugees as temporary exiles from Castro's communism, who would return to their island when he was overthrown. Florida education officials decided to educate the refugee children in their native Spanish and throw in some English for good measure. But when a few thousand refugees grew to hundreds of thousands and a few years to decades, bilingual education became as firmly implanted as a live oak, and has spread nationwide, covering some three million students and growing. Naturally, self-perpetuating bureaucracies within the nation's school systems, most of them funded by the federal government which spends up to $61 million per year *in California alone,* nourishes this growth.

California has more than 1.4 million students who are not fluent in English. After Proposition 227 — effectively ending bilingual education in the nation's most populous state — was passed in 1998 by an overwhelming sixty-one percent of the voters, even many immigrants applauded. Mexican immigrant Eva Castrorena, who had come to the U.S. seven years earlier and is the mother of two sons, thirteen and sixteen, said of Proposition 227, "I supported [it] because the kids need more English. For better education and their future, they need to speak better English. It was very slow with bilingual education. The children learned Spanish not very well and English not very well. I want my sons to go to the university." Bilingual education is a flawed system that often leaves students illiterate in two languages and fluent in none.

An editorial in the *Los Angeles Times,* which had opposed Proposition 227, subsequently gave a surprisingly upbeat assessment of its early consequences:

> The initial results are encouraging, six months after Proposition 227 replaced traditional bilingual education with a nearly exclusive emphasis on English in the classroom.

> Pupils who could barely speak a word of English when school started are acquiring spoken English at a surprising pace, and some are learning to read and write in English . . . The result, no surprise to anyone who has spent any time around young children, is that students are absorbing the English language like a sponge . . . Their success will raise the state's overall student performance. Their failure could cripple their future, and the future of California.

California's battle to replace bilingual education with early English immersion is spreading. Every American should support it. Every American should ignore the charges of racism and nativism coming from ethnic leadership that places short-term political advantage over long-term benefits to immigrants.

Bilingualism, as it slows or stops assimilation, serves to divide, not unite. Once we admit an immigrant, it is both a humanitarian duty and a nationalistic imperative to equip that person to succeed and prosper. The quickest, surest way is the power of English immersion, not the crutch of bilingual education. Our aim should be to Americanize immigrants — not to preserve their status as cultural aliens.

With strong enforcement and resolve, our current legal immigrants can be absorbed into mainstream America.

Illegal aliens are another story. Unbelievably, in 1996, the year of the last official record, the INS estimated the number of illegals in the U.S. at 5,000,000, with 275,000 entering in that year alone. Living in constant fear of discovery and deportation, illegals live a hand-to-mouth existence.

As persons of second-class status, they are denied access to equal protection under our laws because to seek redress for grievances, illegals must contact law enforcement, the last people they want taking notice of them. They cannot vote, they cannot bargain fairly with an employer; they are denied the fundamental rights America stands for. Many have children who share their furtive existence, and while currently educated at taxpayer's expense are helpless pawns in an illegal game.

The 1982 U.S. Supreme Court ruling in Plyler v. Doe says that absent Congressional legislation expressly giving them the power to do so, states cannot deny free, public education to illegal aliens and their children. The court's ruling affected all states, but California took up the cudgel, by fighting back with Proposition 187, which would deny California's illegal immigrants a free education along with all public services except emergency medical care. The sponsor's hope is that 187 will eventually force Congress' hand. President Robert K. Best of the Pacific Legal Foundation, a public interest law firm that feels there is sound legal ground upon which to resurrect 187, wrote: "Specifically, the cost of educating California's illegal alien students for the

1994–1995 school year was estimated at $1.59 billion. Since the average per pupil expenditure in the state was $4,977, this diversion of funds to illegal aliens had a huge impact on lawful residents."

As part of their effort to get the case before the U.S. Supreme Court, the foundation's amicus curiae, with the Ninth Circuit Court, asserted that "At approximately $1.59 billion per year, the funds diverted for three years of educating illegal aliens is more than enough to finance the new classrooms needed to meet the next ten years of California's student population growth." The brief concludes with the argument that "the California electorate made a logical and constitutionally permissible choice" when they overwhelmingly passed Proposition 187. The case is still pending.

We can sugarcoat illegal immigration by sweetening the problem with pleas of economic necessity. The truth is: *Illegal immigration is against the law.* Furthermore, it provides no prospect for a bright future for its children. The illegal existence is only slightly less an affront to civilized behavior than slavery. Illegal immigration is allowed because it either makes money for an employer or builds the constituency for its promoters and apologists. The sooner we come face-to-face with that harsh reality, the sooner we will make a genuine effort to stop it.

The politically correct mantras of multiculturalism and diversity coalesce at the heart of America's assimilation crisis. The idea that assimilation is a dirty word has gained currency in academe, sometimes endorsed by politicians and always vigorously promoted by ethnic elites. The self-aggrandizement of both groups is not a new phenomenon. Politicians need votes; academics need to upset the status quo. As Richard D. Lamm wrote in the October 16, 2000 *Wall Street Journal*, "On most campuses today, a foundation-endowed multicultural circus has driven out the very idea of a common culture, deriding it as a relic of American imperialism."

UCLA's June 1998 commencement was marked by no less than six separate, ethnically based ceremonies. Conducting their own graduations were Hispanics, African-Americans, Filipino-Americans, American Indians, Pacific Islanders, and Iranian Students. Ward Connerly, a Black University of California regent, voiced his dismay over these redundant ceremonies with this cogent question, "Shouldn't graduation day be the one day when all our students regardless of their background can unite as one community? If we are to become one America, we have to examine our conduct and our activities to contribute to that."

Misguided intellectuals within academe, and politically correct politicians share blame for the damage to assimilation done by multiculturalism; also culpable are the so-called ethnic leaders. These activists promote "brown pride," and the restoration of "brown dignity," while rejecting assimilation. These self-styled leaders know they lose influence, one immigrant at a time, as immigrants learn the native language, assimilate and become self-sufficient. So, to maintain power and influence they preach the false gospels of diversity and multiculturalism, while damning assimilation.

We used to unflinchingly demand that immigrants "Americanize," and then help them do it. Now they are told to retain and reinforce their diversity, lest they lose their identity and their heritage. Heritage and identity are givens, and can't be changed any more than the color of the skin or the shape of the eye. But if someone chooses to come to America, he owes it to himself, his children, and his new neighbors to become a part of the whole, not an appendage. At the dinner table she is free to give thanks to whomever she worships, eat tacos or teriyaki, and speak whatever language she chooses, but when she goes out into society she is interacting and competing with English-speaking citizens. Every nuance of language or custom immigrants can master will help them, any deficit hurt them. In the idiom of baseball, why go to bat with two strikes against you when you can start out 0 and 0?

The concept of group rights, so damaging to assimilation, was born of the civil rights movement and consequently enjoys some of its sanctity. Group rights promote the "us v. them" mentality that permeates our society. The virus of victimhood, which is slowly but steadily disappearing among our African-American minority, is becoming an epidemic among some other minority groups.

It's difficult to play "us v. them" without labels and ironically, we, the natives, have created labels for many immigrants in the so-called disadvantaged groups. For instance, the term "Latino" has little meaning to those described. Cubans, Guatemalans, and Mexicans, all considered Latinos, have little more than the Spanish language in common. They come from nations whose histories and cultures are as different as France and Norway, yet we lump them under one ethnic label. The same can be said of the term "Asian." China, Japan, Korea, Laos, and Viet Nam don't even share a common language. Yet, we again assign them a common label so we can identify them as "disadvantaged." Ethnic leaders take advantage of such labeling to push for group rights for their "disadvantaged group."

Examples of group rights abound. Take, for instance, the insistence that admission to our colleges and universities have a strict racial balance, mirroring the racial and ethnic mix of the community. Where this concept is employed as a basis for admission, it ignores ability and hard work in favor of race and ethnicity. It declares that if you are Asian, Hispanic, or Black you will be treated as a disadvantaged minority and granted preference.

Racial set-asides are another example. This practice is employed to insure that a "fair" percentage of government contracts be set aside and granted to minority firms outside the normal competitive bidding process. The definition of "fair" varies from one jurisdiction to another.

An even more fundamental group right is found in the Voting Rights Act of 1965. This piece of legislation essentially guarantees that Blacks and Hispanics today (and who knows what groups in the future) have the right to live in congressional districts in which members of their ethnic groups make up a majority of eligible voters.

The group rights concept provides leverage as various ethnic leaders complain about unequal outcomes, inevitable in a competitive marketplace. When opposition occurs, it is vilified as yet another example of White America's "inherent racism." Author John J. Miller, succinctly stated the group rights problem:

> When the government places a premium on differences and a penalty on commonality, it retards the natural process of assimilation by offering a motive for groups to remain distant from Americanization. It gives them a reason to say they are so unlike everybody else that they cannot possibly be expected to compete on the same playing field, live by the same rules, or conform to the same standards. The result is a poisonous atmosphere of constant suspicion, hostility, and recrimination. It resembles the bitter rivalries of Bosnia, Chechnya, and Rawanda more than the American ideal of E pluribus unum. Today, this problem is almost entirely the creation of government

policy and its system of racial and ethnic classification. It does not occur naturally.

Our nation suffers from immigration indigestion.
Given today's high levels of immigration ingestion, it
will take more than Alka-Seltzer to cure the problem.

Historian Will Durant offered a wise prescription
for the malady when he wrote that, "If Rome had not
engulfed so many men of alien blood in so brief a time, if
she had passed all those newcomers through her schools
instead of her slums, if she had treated them as men
with a hundred potential excellences, if she had occa-
sionally closed her gates to let assimilation catch up with
infiltration, she might have gained new racial and liter-
ary vitality from the infusion, and might have remained
a Roman Rome, the voice and citadel of the West."

10

A New Beginning

The immigration policies of the United States today are deeply flawed because they are driven by economic greed, political opportunism, and the outmoded perception that we should forever conduct ourselves as a nation of immigrants. Whether the problem is porous borders, repeated amnesties for illegal aliens, or agricultural apathy towards a fair wage, we fail to control the overwhelming number of immigrants who desire to reach our shores. As we are diverted by the endless discourse about diversity, human rights, civil rights, group rights, and racial prejudice, the immigrants — legal and illegal — keep crowding through the open door. Our efforts at immigration control are as anachronistic as the corset, as failed as the Edsel.

Fear dominates our politicians' approaches to the subject—fear that by taking a stand on immigration they will alienate one or more of the growing blocks of newly enfranchised immigrant voters. Our political leaders must gather their courage and face reality, the reality that we simply cannot accommodate all those who want to come to America. Where are the political leaders with the courage to face up to that harsh truth and share it with the electorate?

A New Beginning

Our senses dulled by the ether of prosperity, one million people a year were added to our population throughout the 1990s. It now stands at 281 million and is on pace to double in the next sixty years. Allowing this growth to materialize is foolhardy and it must be stopped.

The twelve fastest growing metro areas in the United States during the next twenty years, and the areas that will absorb most of this growth are forecast to be: Atlanta, Phoenix, Houston, Riverside/San Bernardino, San Diego, Los Angeles/Long Beach, Dallas, Washington, D.C., Tampa/St. Petersburg/Clearwater, Denver, Orlando, and Seattle/Bellevue/Everett. If given the opportunity to vote on the subject, it's a near certainty that none of these already crowded areas would step forward and agree to welcome their share of these immigrants. But history tells us these areas are exactly where the vast majority of them will go.

As the leader of the free world, America has heavy responsibilities that must be recognized and accepted. In addition to maintaining our own national security and aiding our allies, these include moral leadership, encouraging respect for human rights, and providing help in times of natural disasters. Absorbing the overpopulation of other nations is not among them.

There are many better ways we can discharge our responsibilities to the community of nations than inviting or, through porous borders, allowing their surplus citizens to move to America. In fact, there is strong evidence that by doing so, over the long run, we actually harm the sending nation's efforts to control its population. Virginia Abernathy, an immigration scholar, asserts that the mere prospect of emigration by excess population "has a pronatalist effect on sending nations, since the opportunity to emigrate causes local population limits to be disregarded."

Another scholar, Garret Hardin, cites studies in *The Immigration Mystique* revealing that:

> ... a decrease in population pressure produces an increase in fertility in animal species ... suggesting that human beings too respond rationally to fluctuations in their populations. We can confidently predict that removing excess fertility from a poor and overpopulated country will produce a rise in fertility.
>
> [Others] argue that emigration, by acting as a safety valve, permits countries with burgeoning populations to postpone controlling these in a manner that would make emigration unnecessary, and is therefore conducive to greater population increase.

Like most controversial issues, many opinions on immigration arise from self-interest or emotion, not facts. A group of four articles on the pros and cons of immigration in the February 3, 1999, *San Francisco Examiner* featured Peter King, a columnist, who opined sentimentally and nostalgically that California would "lose its spirit and soul" if it did not offer haven for all immigrants wanting to settle in the already most populous state. Another contributor, Congressman Martin Frost of Texas declared that legal immigrants did not supplant the native workforce, but supplemented it.

Fortunately, these unrealistic notions were brought to earth with an article by Terry Anderson, a self-employed mechanic from South-Central Los Angeles. Anderson lamented that Black teenagers in his area couldn't get after-school or entry-level jobs without knowing Spanish, that when he was a teenager, he had jobs at McDonald's, Burger King and Jack-in-the-Box. In the late 1970s, he wrote, he sold parts to auto body shops, and knew American guys who were making $20 an hour repairing dented fenders. Now, he concluded, ninety-five percent of body shop jobs are held by recent immigrants making $7 to $8 an hour.

Anderson lashed out at Black politicians, who, he said, are in favor of more immigration, while ignoring the complaints of their Black constituents who feel they are being pushed aside by the high number of immigrants crowding into their neighborhoods. Anderson recommended a five-year immigration moratorium.

The fourth contributor to the debate was B. Meredith Burke, immigration author and senior fellow with Negative Population Growth in Washington, D.C. She wrote that when a state or nation lets its population grow above the "carrying capacity" level it sets itself on the path to ecological self-destruction. She feels that the nation has continued on this path despite a 1972 presidential commission that urged the U.S. to move with all possible speed to stabilize its then population of 200 million, which the commission called "already ecologically unsustainable."

In a *Washington Post* letter to the editor, Kathleen McNeilly of Carrying Capacity Network in Washington, D.C., says, in a tongue-in-cheek rebuttal of the stance that we need to accept more and more newcomers: "Traffic too light for you? Water and air too clean? Open space too abundant? National Parks too empty? Don't worry, the population growth and mass immigration that [immigration enthusiasts] endorse will soon take care of these deficiencies."

Perhaps America's most clear-eyed observer of immigration is the former three-term governor of Colorado, Democrat Richard D. Lamm, who insists that immigration policies and attitudes that served the U.S. well in the early part of the twentieth century are no longer valid in the twenty-first. Governor Lamm, a prolific author on immigration, wrote in 1999 that we have been blinded by past immigration successes, and in the newly emerged paradigm we must understand that economic theories cannot be at variance with ecological reality.

In one of Lamm's articles, "The Culture of Growth and the Culture of Limits," he cites an Emile Zola story in which a trainload of soldiers on the way to war is rushing downhill, the driver and fireman fighting over whether to stoke the engine or not. As the two men tussle, they tumble off the engine, leaving the partying soldiers hurtling through the night on an unmanned train, totally unaware of what is happening. The U.S., like the train, is running out of control down a track to disaster from inattention to immigration policies and numbers.

It's inevitable that some people question the relevancy, even the viability of the concept of "nation." Not so with Alexander Solzhenitsyn, the Russian writer and Nobel Prize winner. He declared that, "the disappearance of nations would impoverish us no less than if all peoples were made alike, with one character, one face." The issue deserves our attention here because it is central to any discussion of immigration. Successful immigration policy must recognize the primacy of nations, ours and others; each one different from the other, each one proud in its own way of its singular contributions to world culture.

David S. Landes, in his seminal work, *The Wealth and Poverty of Nations*, celebrates the importance of nationhood to one of the world's oldest:

> Britain had the early advantage of being a
> *nation*. By that I mean not simply the realm of
> a ruler, not simply a state or political entity, but
> a self-conscious, self-aware unit characterized

by common identity and loyalty and by equality of civil status. Nations can reconcile social purpose with individual aspirations and initiatives and enhance performance by their collective synergy. The whole is more than the sum of the parts.

The idea of a "one world" or borderless society is a delusion. Nations are fundamental to social structure. The borders of nations, contrived and illogical as some may be, serve an indispensable purpose. They define where the jurisdiction of one nation ends and another's begins. As the European Union develops, its progress should not be seen as diminishing the importance of nations but rather a simplification of the rules of national interrelationships. The French and English — the Chunnel notwithstanding — are not about to join hands and march off under a common flag, speak a common language, and share a common ethos. Neither are Swedes and Danes, Italians and Austrians, Spaniards and Portuguese.

As proof of the continuing importance of nationhood, our world, particularly in the last 100 years, has seen a steep increase in the number of nations. *Hammond's 1999 Centennial World Atlas* lists 192 independent nations. The oldest claim to nationhood is Japan's, which dates back to 660 B.C. The newest is the island of Palau, which became an independent nation in 1994. Many nations are hundreds, or like Japan, even thousands of years old, yet thirty-six were born in the first half of the twentieth century and 109 in the second half. While much of this growth is attributable to the deaths of colonialism and the Soviet Union, it still bears witness to people's innate drive to organize and belong. Compare the feelings of identity and belonging of a person who is simply a citizen of the world to one who knows he is an American, a Swiss, or even a Canadian who wants to become a Quebecois.

Canada aside, the world today is witness to several other concurrent separatist movements and wars of liberation. People are fighting, and, in some cases dying, for the right to form still more independent nations. It is clear that both human nature and the sweep of history take us toward more, not fewer nations. Tribalism is alive and well in the twenty-first century.

Every nation, old or new, has its own set of needs and priorities that should be reflected in its immigration laws. To be meaningful, these laws, as much as the borders defining a nation, must be enforced. If they are not, the nation, any nation, will soon lose its relevancy and be swallowed by its neighbor. As tribalism is alive and well, so is the law of the jungle. Passive nations and inert individuals both invite irrelevancy.

Our staunch Canadian allies, like us, have wrestled with the immigration issue for generations and for many of the same reasons. They, too, started with a vast frontier needing immigrants to help settle it. Until recently Canada had a quite liberal attitude toward immigration. In 1997, the country admitted many more immigrants in proportion to its population than Australia or the U.S.

But in the 1990s, Canada's most popular urban areas, those that attracted the most immigrants, attained a population density and ethnic transformation sufficient to cause many Canadians to say "enough!" (Or, in French-speaking, secessionist Quebec, "ca suffit.") Responding to the public will, Canada's Parliament made some fundamental changes to immigration policy. Realizing the need for a healthy dose of self-interest in immigration policy, it devised a point-scoring system — where the maximum number was 100 — awarding each potential immigrant points based on what was best for Canada at any given time. Part of this equation is Canada's unemployment rate at the time of application. Recognizing that all provinces do not have the same employment needs at the same time, Canada allows an immigrant to apply for admission either to a particular province or to Canada at large. For those with a provincial preference, the scoring system is modified to provide that province a voice in the selection process. The nuclear family is admitted or rejected as an entity, thereby avoiding the family reunification issue.

All potential immigrants are given Canada's *Guide for Independent Applicants,* which begins with this caution: "The most important factor is your intended occupation, i.e., the occupation in which you have experience and are qualified, and which you are prepared to follow in Canada. A number of other selection factors, including experience and the education and training factor are based upon this occupation."

The application packet for all potential immigrants contains Canada's current list of occupations and the assigned point value for each. Those in short supply carry a higher point value. The guide enumerates all other characteristics upon which the immigrant will be judged, again indicating the point value for each. It is made clear that if the applicant scores less than sixty points, "your application may not merit further consideration."

Age is graded highest (10 points) for those from 21 to 44 years old. Those under 17 or over 48 are given a sobering zero. Those without a high school diploma receive no points; those with a diploma are awarded 10. Higher education earns up to 16 points for a Ph.D. A pre-arranged job, properly verified, is worth 10 points. Fluency in either English or French will earn the applicant 9 points, with a bonus of up to 6 points for partial or full command of a second language. Five points are granted to those having Canadian relatives.

One of Canada's grading features, the demographic factor, is rife with possibilities for creative immigration management in the U.S. A maximum of 8 points are awarded on the basis of Canada's current rate of unemployment. More points are awarded in times of low unemployment. The number of points can be increased or decreased to further the country's immediate immigration objectives.

Canada will not accept indigent immigrants. Candidates are told up front: "All independent applicants must also prove they have enough money to support themselves and their dependents for at least six months after they arrive in Canada." As a guide, an independent applicant is usually expected to have at least $10,000 Canadian dollars plus $2,000 Canadian dollars for each dependent.

Finally, the entire family must pass physical examinations. Anyone with a physical condition which is "a danger to public health or safety or would cause excessive demand on health or social services in Canada," is rejected. Once admitted, immigrants immediately become permanent legal residents and are eligible for most social benefits accorded Canadian citizens, except the right to vote. After they meet the residency requirement (currently thirty-six of the last forty-eight months in Canada) and other requirements, they may apply for citizenship.

Canada's intelligent approach to managing immigration shapes the flow of immigrants to fit Canada's national interest. By contrast, our policy has family reunification as its central theme. This is a "feel good" approach to a complex issue and ignores America's needs. It has resulted in runaway population growth fueled by immigrants and their relatives — nuclear and otherwise.

Foreign relations, national defense, welfare, and civil rights law are examples of vital areas of public policy, but they pale in comparison to immigration and the impact runaway population has on our everyday lives.

A New Beginning

Because of the singular importance of the immigration problem and the failure of the legislative process to deal effectively with it, immigration policy should become a special case, conducted forcefully in the national interest and free from the debilitating influence of special interests.

There is a device in American policy making that can help bring this about. Used in twenty-six states including California, it's called the "initiative." Its purpose is to give citizens at voting time a method of informing their state legislature of their wishes on matters to which the legislature has been unresponsive to the public will, exactly the case we have at the national level regarding immigration policy. The device could be expanded and used as a vehicle for direct public input to each state's congressional delegation. Here is what a ballot measure would look like in a typical state:

INSTRUCTIONS TO CONGRESS
REGARDING IMMIGRATION

1. The number of immigrants allowed into this state in each of the next four years should be: *(choose one)*

   ❐ none
   ❐ 1,000
   ❐ 10,000
   ❐ 100,000
   ❐ unlimited

2. Their minimum education level should be:
   (choose one)
   - ☐ no minimum
   - ☐ kindergarten through eighth grade attendance
   - ☐ high school graduate
   - ☐ college graduate
   - ☐ college post-graduate degree

3. Instruct the Immigration and Naturalization Service to rank the following qualities of applicants from one to five as indicated. *One being the most important and five the least:*
   The rank this voter assigns is:
   - ☐ Education
   - ☐ Family connections here
   - ☐ Our need for their vocation
   - ☐ Financial ability to create jobs here
   - ☐ Financial ability to be self-sustaining

Note that there is no question regarding race, ethnicity, or country of origin. None of those factors should be involved in selecting immigrants; instead the focus is on what the voter wants newcomers to bring to his or her state. How will the immigrant contribute to our society? Does he or she practice a vocation we need? What is the voter's opinion about the number of immigrants we should admit during the next four years? These are the questions we want answers to — questions that will guide Congress in the formulation of focused, purposeful immigration policy, responsive to the will of each state's people. The power of today's many pressure groups will be greatly diminished when Congress knows the immigration wishes and priorities of their constituents.

Some will ask, "Why not just conduct public opinion polls?" The answer is that people don't trust them. We often hear complaints that they are never called during such polls. Another common criticism is that due to manipulation of some questions and how they are phrased, the point of view of those who pay for the poll usually prevails.

The use of the initiative device every four years would provide all voting citizens with a means to help decide the quantity and composition of who is allowed into the U.S. These results would serve to guide the INS on the qualifications and number of immigrants each state would willingly accept. Passage of a federal law mandating the vote would be necessary.

This book has suggested pertinent fixes to our present immigration policy. Even if those were to go into effect tomorrow, it could take decades for our present immigrants to meld into the larger society, to assimilate and to pass on to their children the best of the values of American society as they are commonly understood. That's too long. A more drastic solution is needed, a bold one, but with only the good of the country in mind. The crisis caused by the ascending curve of immigrants during the 1990s cries out for an immediate "time-out" for assimilation, acculturation, and the thoughtful development of future immigration policy. What does it say about us when our ecology is suffering a major stroke? Or that we endure unprecedented crowding of our cities? Or helplessly watch our school system in chronic breakdown? Are we only interested in perpetuating sentimental aphorisms about the open door, created when we were a country with wide-open spaces, into the present where the absence of cell phone babble is considered a luxury?

The United States needs ten years of near zero immigration to absorb and acculturate its present overpopulation. This moratorium will provide time to acculturate our newest arrivals, time for them to absorb the traditions and attitudes that, since the birth of our nation, have transformed immigrants into Americans. Abraham Lincoln described the process as one that unites us through the power of "mystic chords of memory, stretching from battlefield and patriot grave to every living heart and hearthstone all over this broad land." During this ten-year moratorium, we could bring legal immigration down to nothing and better control illegal immigration. During the ten-year period, we could carefully decide what immigration course we wish to chart for the future, what rate of immigration will most benefit America, and what qualities and talents we are looking for in our immigrants.

What else will the moratorium accomplish? Above all, a blessing for our underclass. Increased opportunities and income will attract people into the work force who now find welfare or unemployment compensation more lucrative than work. Opportunity and upward mobility will replace futility and hopelessness. This improved outlook will also reduce the severity of much social pathology — crime, drug abuse, babies having babies, fatherless homes, and poverty. When the inflow of cheap labor is ended, there will be a growth of job opportunities and increased incomes, as wages rise to reflect the true economic value of entry-level jobs. Will we have to pay more for some goods and services with the rise in wages of entry-level jobs? Of course, but we will have traded human misery for opportunity, an ennobling transaction by any standard.

The assertion that "Americans simply won't do the low-wage, entry-level jobs immigrants do" is specious. How did those jobs get done before the onset of massive immigration? If further affirmation is needed, go to some of the cities in our heartland that haven't yet felt the full impact of out-of-control immigration. They get their dishes washed, their lawns mowed, and their burgers flipped. Perhaps they pay a little more to get it done, and so should the rest of us. Thousands of unemployed and under-employed Americans would find their way into the work force, if entry-level work were more remunerative and working conditions less onerous.

Politicians are at pains not to tie immigration growth to the widening gap between rich and poor in America. But economists such as Jeffery G. Williamson and

Peter H. Lindert have observed that this gap has been at its widest during times of peak immigration. After World War I, when immigration to the U.S. was cut off, the disparity between rich and poor narrowed. In earlier years, the periods of 1820 to 1860 and the 1890s to World War I, economic inequality worsened as more immigrants arrived. Allowing free market equilibrium to determine labor costs will improve the circumstances of the poor without severely impacting the rest of society.

Bringing about seriously decreased immigration will require reevaluation of our fixation on continuous, straight-line economic growth in the U.S. From a mantra for our national agenda, to the be-all and end-all of American political and social policy formulation, the pursuit of economic growth has dominated our country for decades. Alan Greenspan, Chairman of the Federal Reserve, sees his primary objective as boosting economic growth, and has remained our economic Louis XIV through presidents of both parties, all who fear that after him would come the *déluge*.

From John Kennedy's "We must get America moving again," to the federal price controls of Nixon, to Clinton's "It's the economy, stupid," U.S. voters have rewarded politicians who equate economic growth with life, liberty, and the pursuit of happiness. The relentless quest for individual affluence has spawned homes where both parents feel the need to work "to provide more," where "latchkey kids" are symbols of the decline of parenting, and vacations are taken at sites where beauty, tranquility, and open space are but vague memories.

Allowing millions of immigrants to come here in the name of economic growth while adding to overcrowding and decreasing our quality of life is just another manifestation of the pursuit of affluence at all costs. We need to reassess our national priorities. We need a larger purpose than ever-increasing material wealth. America should strive to surpass previous generations in its quality of life; the purity of its air and water, the unfettered flow of its traffic, the beauty, profusion, and proximity of open space, the excellence of education, and the abundance of opportunity at all socioeconomic levels. These are the values that count. These are the values that will make us a greater, if not necessarily a materially wealthier nation. The realization of all these values is deterred by today's excessive immigration.

As citizens of the world's most diverse nation, we *can* rid ourselves of the destructive immigration practices that have come at the expense of our present and future psychic and physical well-being. This transformation must start with natives and immigrants alike, both groups understanding and vigorously opposing the folly of our present immigration laws and demanding a new beginning. Changing America's lodestar to improving the quality of life for all people will provide our nation with a bright new beacon by which to navigate in the twenty-first century.

BIBLIOGRAPHY

The following Web sites are valuable resources of information:

University of California at Berkeley: http://www.berkeley.edu/about/.
The full text of Stephen Legomsky's paper, "Quotas and Preferences in United States Immigration Law," is available on the Web at: http://www.uni-konstanz.de/FuF/ueberfak/fzaa/alt/mpf/mpfl/mpfl-legomsky.html.
"Guide for Independent Applicants," July 1999, on the Canadian government's Web site is available at: http://cicnet.ci.gc.ca/english/immigr/guide-ce.html.

Unless otherwise indicated, all references to the operations of the San Diego border patrol operation are based on personal interviews with Border Patrol Agents, Mario Villarreal, Roy Villareal (SIC), and Marc S. Jackson, in San Diego, California on February 18, 2000.

Alchorn, Louis. *Creating Bosnia in America.* Pittsburgh, Pennsylvania: Dorrance Publishing Co. Inc., 1995.

Bibliography

Anderson, Stuart. "The Effect of Immigrant Scientists and Engineers on Wages and Employment in High Technology." In *The Debate in the United States Over Immigration*, Peter Duignan and Lewis H. Gann, eds. Stanford, California: Hoover Institution Press, 1998.

Asimov, Nanette. "Prop. 227 Challenged in Lawsuit." *San Francisco Chronicle*, June 4, 1998.

Backgrounder. "Distorted Incentives — The United States Pays the University of California Twice as Much to Educate Foreign Graduate Students as American Ones." Washington, D.C.: Center for Immigration Studies, February 2000.

Ballon, Marc. "U.S. High-Tech Jobs Going Abroad." *Los Angeles Times*, April 24, 2000.

Barlett, Donald L., and James B. Steele. *America: Who Stole The Dream?* Kansas City, Missouri: Andrews and McMeel, 1996.

Barnes, Carla. *Fresno County and Sub-County Average Annual Unemployment Rates, 1999.* State of California Employment Development Department, Fresno, California.

Bartley, Robert L. "Liberty's Flame Beckons a Bit Brighter." *Wall Street Journal*, July 3, 2000.

Beck, Roy. *The Case Against Immigration.* New York: W. W. Norton & Co., 1996.

————. "The High Cost of Cheap Foreign Labor." In *The Debate in the United States Over Immigration*, Peter Duignan and L. H. Gann, eds. Stanford, California: Hoover Institute Press, 1998.

———. *Re-charting America's Future.* Petosky, Michigan: The Social Contract Press, 1994.

Beltrame, Julian. "Canada's Yawning Need for Immigrants Grows." *Wall Street Journal,* July 10, 2000.

Best, Robert K. President of the Pacific Legal Foundation, in a letter to this author, May 10, 2000.

Borjas, George J. "Immigration, the Issue-in-Waiting." *New York Times,* April 2, 1999.

———. "Immigration and Welfare." In *The Debate in the United States Over Immigration.* Peter Duignan and Lewis H. Gann, eds. Stanford, California: Hoover Institution Press, 1998.

———. "Mexico's One-Way Remedy." *New York Times,* July 18, 2000.

Branigan, William. "House Sets Aside Bill to Allow Hiring of More Foreign Workers." *Washington Post,* August 1, 1998.

Briggs, Vernon M., Jr., and Stephen Moore. *Still An Open Door?* Washington, D.C.: The American University Press, 1994.

Brimelow, Peter. *Alien Nation.* New York: Harper Collins, 1996.

Browne, Sharon L., Mark T. Gallagher, Stephen R. McCutcheon, Jr. "Brief Amicus Curiae in the United States Court of Appeals for the Ninth Circuit, in the matter of: League of United Latin American Citizens et al. v. Pete Wilson, Governor of the State of California." Sacramento, California: The Pacific Legal Foundation, 1998.

Bibliography

Camarota, Steven. "Our New Immigration Predicament." *The American Enterprise,* December 2000.

Camarota, Steven A., and Mark Krikorian. "A Myth Dies Hard." *National Review,* February 21, 2000.

Castro, Max J., ed. *Free Markets, Open Societies, Closed Borders.* Miami, Florida: North-South Center Press at the University of Miami, 1999.

Chao, Julie. "S. F. Flyers Preach Hate, Alarm Chinese Americans." *San Francisco Examiner,* July 21, 1999.

Colon, Yves. "Colombia Insurgency Fueling Exodus." *Miami Herald,* November 24, 1998.

———. "INS Hiring 25 Officers to Speed Up Naturalizations." *Miami Herald,* March 16, 1999.

Crossette, Barbara. "Testing the Limits of Tolerance as Cultures Mix." *New York Times,* March 6, 1999.

Cunha, Jr., Manuel. Mr. Cunha was interviewed by the author in Mr. Cunha's Fresno, California office on April 2, 2000. All references to Mr. Cunha and the Nisei Farmers League are based on that interview.

D'Souza, Dinesh. *The Virtue of Prosperity.* New York: The Free Press, 2000.

de Cordoba, Jose. "As Violence Worsens, Business Leaders Flee Colombia, Venezuela." *The Wall Street Journal,* August 30, 2000.

del Olmo, Frank. "Latinos Want Substance in the Form of Amnesty." *Los Angeles Times,* August 15, 2000.

Dillon, Sam. "Mexico Weighs Voting By Its Emigrants In U.S." *New York Times,* December 7, 1998.

Donnelly, Paul. "Indefinitely Temporary." Center For Immigration Studies *Backgrounder* (March 2000).

Duignan, Peter and L. H. Gann, eds. *The Debate in the United States Over Immigration* (Stanford, CA: Hoover Institution Press, 1998).

———— *The Spanish Speakers in the United States.* Lanham, Maryland: University Press of America, 1998.

The Economist. "Mexico — Let Them Eat Hamburgers." January 9, 1999.

———— . "Female Genital Mutilation — Is it Crime or Culture?" February 13, 1999.

———— . "Politics and Silicon Valley," October 30, 1999.

———— . "The Assault on Democratic Society in Colombia." March 18, 2000.

———— . "Canada — Votes and Immigrants." June 10, 2000.

———— . "California's Power Crisis." January 20, 2001.

Fine, Howard. "State Sets Up Bank for Infrastructure Improvement." *The Los Angeles Business Journal,* December 17, 1995.

Freedberg, Louis, and Ramon G. McLeod. "The Other Side of the Law." *San Francisco Chronicle,* October 13, 1998.

Gimpel, James G., and James R. Edwards, Jr. *The Congressional Politics of Immigration Reform,* Needham Heights, Massachusetts: Allyn & Bacon, 1999.

Gotz-Richter, Stephan, and Daniel Bachman. "Welcome More Immigrants." *Wall Street Journal,* July 22, 1998.

Bibliography

Greenhouse, Steven. "Guess Who's Embracing Immigrants Now." *New York Times*, March 5, 2000.

Gross, Martin L. *The End Of Sanity.* New York: Avon Books, 1997.

Grover, James, and Paul G. Huray. "Boom May Bust Engineers." *San Francisco Chronicle,* September 21, 1998.

Hailbronner, Kay, David A. Martin, and Hiroshi Motomura, eds. *Immigration Admissions — The Search for Workable Policies in Germany and the United States.* Providence, Rhode Island: Berghahn Books, 1997.

Hammond 1999 Centennial World Atlas. "Population." Maplewood, New Jersey: Hammond.

————. "World Flags and Reference Guide." Ibid.

Harwood, Edwin. *In Liberty's Shadow.* Stanford, California: Hoover Institution Press, 1986.

Harwood, John. "Courting Hispanics, the New Soccer Moms of Politics." *Wall Street Journal,* October 15, 1999.

Hedges, Stephen J. "The Border Town Middlemen." *U.S. News & World Report,* September 23, 1996.

Hesburgh, Theodore M. U.S. Select Commission on Immigration and Refugee Policy, Final Report: U.S. Immigration Policy and the National Interest, Washington, D.C.: U.S. Government Printing Office, 1981.

Hu, Winnie. *"Woman Fearing Mutilation Savors Freedom." New York Times,* August 20, 1999.

Huspek, Michael. "Give Some Coyotes a Break." *Los Angeles Times,* July 5, 1998.

Jasso, Guillermina, and Mark R. Rosenzweig, *The New*

Chosen People: Immigrants in the United States. New York: Russell Sage Foundation, 1990.

———. "Family Reunification and the Immigration Multiplier: U.S. Immigration Law, Origin Country Conditions, and the Reproduction of Immigrants." *Demography,* Volume 23, Number 3, August, 1986.

Johnson, Bryan T., Kim R. Holmes, and Melanie Kirkpatrick. *1999 Index of Economic Freedom.* Washington, D.C.: The Heritage Foundation; New York: Dow Jones and Company. 1999.

Johnson, John, and Deborah Sullivan Brennan. "$21 Million Deal to Improve Farm Worker Housing." *Los Angeles Times,* May 23, 2000.

Karkabi, Barbara. "Special Day Honors the Oppressed." *Houston Chronicle,* December 7, 1998.

Kifner, John. "Scientists Say Pakistani Defector Is Not Credible." *New York Times,* July 8, 1998.

Kiplinger, Knight. *World Boom Ahead.* Washington, D.C.: The Kiplinger Washington Editors, Inc., 1998.

Kiplinger Washington Letter, October 23, 1998, p. 3.

Lamm, Richard D. "The Culture of Growth and the Culture of Limits." *The Social Contract,* Spring 1999.

———. "Big Plans, Harmful Results." *Wall Street Journal,* October 16, 2000.

Lamm, Richard D., and Gary Imhoff. *The Immigration Time Bomb.* New York: Truman Talley Books, 1985.

Landes, David S. *The Wealth and Poverty of Nations.* New York: W. W. Norton & Company, 1998.

Lee, Kenneth K. *Huddled Masses, Muddled Laws.* Westport, Connecticut: Praeger Publishers, 1998.

Legomsky, Stephen H. Paper presented November 10, 1997, in Bonn, Germany. "Quotas and Preferences in United States Immigration Law." All references to the Immigration and Naturalization Act of 1952, except where noted, are based on his paper. The full text of the paper is available on the Web at http://www.uni-konstanz.de/FuF/ueberfak/fzaa/alt/mpf/mpfl/mpfl-legomsky.html.

Levy, Doug. "High-tech Firms Hope for Higher Cap on Worker Visas." *USA Today,* September 21, 1998.

Loaeza, Enrique M., and Susan Martin, *Binational Study on Migration Between Mexico and the United States.* Washington, D.C.: U.S. Commission on Immigration Reform, 1997.

Los Angeles Times. Editorial. "Re-think Border Crossing Plan." February 6, 1998.

Lucatero, Cecilia. The author interviewed Cecilia Lucatero in Palos Verdes, California on October 10, 2000.

Machalaba, Daniel. "As Economy Hums, Congested Freeways Exact a Heavy Toll." *Wall Street Journal,* August 30, 2000.

Markley, Melanie. "Hispanics Say Student's Rights Being Violated." *Houston Chronicle,* August 21, 1998.

Martin, Philip L. "The Endless Debate." In *The Debate in the United States Over Immigration,* Peter Duignan and Lewis H. Gann, eds. Stanford, California: Hoover Institution Press, 1998.

———. "Guest Worker Programs for the 21st Century." Washington, D.C.: Center For Immigration Studies, *Backgrounder,* April 2000.

Marx, Gary, and Teresa Puente. "Latin Kings Prey on Need for Illegal Documents." *Chicago Tribune,* September 19, 1999.

Masters, Brooke A., and Sylvia Moreno, "Fraud Flourishes as Immigrants Seek Help." *Washington Post,* July 21, 1998.

McCarthy, Kevin F., and Georges Vernez. *Immigration in a Changing Economy — California's Experience.* Santa Monica, California: RAND, 1997.

McDonnell, Patrick J. "Asylum-Seekers Held Long Periods Despite Clean Records." *Los Angeles Times,* September 9, 1998.

―――. "Davis Won't Appeal Prop. 187." *Los Angeles Times,* July 29, 1999.

―――. "Mexican Arrivals Seek New Frontiers." *Los Angeles Times,* June 19, 1997.

McNeilly, Kathleen. Letter to the Editor. *Washington Post,* July 28, 1998.

Miller, John, J. "Can't We Do a Better Job of 'Americanizing' Immigrants?" *Houston Chronicle,* May 31, 1998.

―――. *The Unmaking of America.* New York: The Free Press, 1998.

Morello, Carol. "Little Desert Town Is New Immigrant Battleground." *USA Today,* July 21, 1999.

Mujica, Mauro E. "An Open Letter to Members of U.S. English." July 9, 1999. [Mr. Mujica is the president of U.S. English.]

Nakamura, David. "Loudoun School Rule Criticized." *Washington Post,* September 25, 1998.

Bibliography

Nelson, Brent A. *America Balkanized.* (Monterey, Virginia: American Immigration Control Foundation, 1994.

New York Times. "Backlog Reduces Grants of Legal Residence." August 12, 1999.

Newmyer, Jacqueline. "Rights Group Says 5 Areas Poised for Tragedy." *Los Angeles Times,* June 15, 2000.

O'Sullivan, John. "Silicon Implants." *National Review,* June 1, 1998.

Pagano, Michael A. "Trends in Infrastructure Funding: The Other Year 2000 Problem." *Government Finance Review,* December 1998.

Pear, Robert. "Accord Would Increase Cap on Visas for Skilled Workers." *New York Times,* July 25, 1998.

Perlstein, Linda. "Tough Subject: Lowering Latino Dropout rate. *Washington Post,* December 1, 1998.

Pollock, Dennis, and Robert Rodriquez. "Changes Grow in Agriculture. *Fresno Bee,* April 8, 2000.

Rector, Robert. "A Retirement Home For Immigrants." *Wall Street Journal,* February 20, 1996.

Ritter, John. "Growers Push Plan to Legalize Workers." *USA Today,* November 19, 1999.

Robinson, Andrea. "Cuban Exile Protest Called Self Indulgent." *Miami Herald,* July 1, 1999.

Rubin, Barry R. *The Citizens Guide to Politics in America.* Armonk, New York: M. E. Sharpe, 1997.

Samuelson, Robert J. "The Limits of Immigration" *Newsweek,* July 24, 2000.

Bibliography

Sanchez, Rene, and William Booth. "California's Rejection a Big Blow to Bilingualism." *Washington Post*, June 4, 1998.

Schiller, Dane. "Texas is Seeing More Migration, Deaths at Border." *San Antonio Express News,* December 14, 1998.

Schippers, David. "Injustice for All." Washington, D.C.: Center for Immigration Studies, *Backgrounder,* October 2000.

Schneider, Dick. "Big Growth a Threat to California." *San Francisco Chronicle,* January 17, 1999.

————. Telephone interview with Dick Schneider, April 18, 2000.

Schoeni, Robert, Kevin F. McCarthy, and Georges Vernez. *The Mixed Economic Progress of Immigrants.* Santa Monica, California: RAND, 1996.

Smith, Diane, and Andrew Backover. "Working Around the Law." *Fort Worth Texas Star-Telegram,* April 18, 1999.

Smith, James F. "Mexico's Dual Nationality Opens Doors." *Los Angeles Times,* March 20, 1998.

Smith, Lamar. Letter to the Editor. *Washington Post,* February 16, 1998.

Sontag, Deborah, and Celia W. Dugger. "The New Immigrant Tide: A Shuttle Between Worlds." *New York Times,* July 19, 1998.

Taylor, J. Edwards, Philip L. Martin, and Michael Fix. *Poverty Amid Prosperity,* Washington, D.C.: The Urban Institute Press, 1997.

Bibliography

U.S. Department of Justice, Immigration and Naturalization Service. "Fact Sheet — Public Charge." May 25, 1999.

U.S. Immigration and Naturalization Service, 1998 *Statistical Yearbook of the Immigration and Naturalization Service,* Washington, D.C.: U.S. Government Printing Office, 2000.

Valbrun, Marjorie. "Senate Approves Raising Number of H-1B Visas." *Wall Street Journal,* October 4, 2000.

Van Natta, Jr., Don. "Republicans Open a Big Drive to Appeal to Hispanic Voters." *New York Times,* January 15, 2000.

Vernez, Georges, and Allan Abrahamse. *How Immigrants Fare in U.S. Education.* Santa Monica, California: RAND, 1996.

Viglucci, Andres. "Agencies Discuss Stepping Up Fight Against Alien Smuggling." *Miami Herald,* October 2, 1998.

Wall Street Journal. "Canadian Commuters Face Traffic Jams Crossing The Border." March 17, 1998.

――― . "Casting The Net." March 7, 2000.

――― . "Free the Roads." April 21, 2000.

Wallace, Jim. "Unconventional Thoughts." *Los Angeles Times,* August 15, 2000.

Ward, Barbara. *The Rich Nations and the Poor Nations.* New York: W. W. Norton & Company, 1962.

Weiss, Kenneth R. "Mixing Commencement and Culture." *Los Angeles Times,* June 20, 1998.

Bibliography

Westphal, Sylvia Pagan. "Fighting the Fakes." *Los Angeles Times,*" February 11, 2000.

Wickham, DeWayne. "Try Harder to Hire U.S. Tech Workers." *USA Today,* August 13, 1998.

Wilgoren, Jodi. "Electronic Wall Going Up Along the Borders." *Los Angeles Times,* March 17, 1998.

Williams, Molly. "AuthenTec Sees Wide Use for Fingerprint ID." *Wall Street Journal,* December 14, 2000.

Williamson, Jr., Chilton. *The Immigration Mystique.* New York: Basic Books, 1996.

Wright, Robin. "World Population Reaches 6 Billion." *Los Angeles Times,* May 17, 1999.

Zitner, Aaron "More Visas for Workers Are Sought." *Boston Globe, March 8, 1998.*

INDEX

acculturation, 146

AFL – CIO: endorsement of amnesty for illegals; 26, 29, 47, 83

Agriculture: reliance on immigrant labor, 45; seeks cheap labor, 47; workers sub-standard housing, 48–49

Alaska, 58–59

Americanization, 128, 146

amnesty, 26, 60, 81–82

Arizona: Cochise County, 103; Douglas, 102; Nogales, 100; Phoenix, 9

Asian immigrants, 21, 41

Assimilation: America's capacity for, not unlimited, 116; diminished by bi-lingual education, 122; electronic devices make it less important to immigrants, 109–110; essential to successful immigration, 113–114; huge numbers make it more difficult, 110, 115; missing from ancient Rome, 131; naturalization is ultimate act of, 108; problems for illegals, 126; time-out for, 146–147

asylum, 73, 75

balance of resolve, 105–106

Balkanization, 116

ballots in multiple languages, 120–122

Beck, Roy, 6, 10, 17, 56

bi-lingual education, began with Cubans, 122; masquerades as friend of immigrants, 122

biometrics, 99

Black Americans, ix, 1, 19,

Black politicians, 135

bonding of financial sponsors, 67–68

Border control operations: Gate-keeper, 100; Safeguard, 100; Hold the Line, 100; Rio Grande, 100

Border Patrol, 46, 93–94, 101–102

Bracero Program, 50–51

brown pride/dignity, 127–128

Brownsville, Texas, 100

Bush, George W., 81

California: cost of bi-lingual education in, 123; employers pay immigrants less, 58; Employment Development Department, 71; energy crisis, 9; ethnic composition of, 4; Fresno County, 52; Highland Park, 111;

Index

California (*continued*)
    Mexican population in Los
        Angeles, 115; illegal alien's
        babies born in, 117; over-
        crowded schools, 13; population
        growth, 10; Riverside County
        farm workers housing, 48–49;
        San Diego, 100-101
Canada: approach to immigration,
    139–142; U.S. border with, 103;
    illegal aliens enter from, 103
Carrying Capacity Network,
    135–136
Castro, Fidel, 89
Caucasians, ix
Center for Immigration Studies, 41
chain immigration: babies of illegal
    alien mothers start, 117;
    defined, 57; delayed action of,
    60; should be ended, 62
cheap labor: H-1B visas help
    supply, 35; inflow stopped by
    moratorium, 147
Chesapeake Bay, 5
China: one child policy, 75; Mus-
    lim persecution in, 79
Chinese-Americans, 14
Citizenship (U.S.): efforts to speed
    process in time for 1996 elec-
    tion, 119; *for babies born to illegal
    parents in U.S., 117;* oath of,
    113; requirements for, 118
civil rights, 132
Clinton, William J., 4
Coast Guard, U.S., 16, 75
Colombia, 74, 79, 88
Colorado, 9
common language, 108
Communist controlled countries, 78

computer science graduates, 35
Congress: attempt to correct racial
    inequities in immigration, 21;
    authorizes too few enforcers, 69;
    can be bypassed, 118; considers
    further amnesty, 47; ethno-cen-
    tric members of, 25, 26; guides
    for, in initiative ballot, 143–145;
    lobbied to grant more H-1B
    visas, 33–36; recognizes prob-
    lem, 57; repeated amnesties
    passed by, 85; strengthens INS's
    hand, 67; support low for
    increasing immigration, 29
Connerly, Ward, 127
constituency building, 26
counterfeit documents, 70–72,
    96–98
country of origin, should not be a
    factor in immigration policy,
    144
Cubans, 15, 74, 89
cultural differences, 114–115

Davis, Gray, 31
disadvantaged groups, 129
Displaced Persons Act of 1948, 77
Diversity: coalesced with multi-
    culturalism, 126–127; discourse
    about, 132; object of one pro-
    gram, 23; as alternative to
    assimilation, 127–128
dual citizenship: for Mexicans,
    112; other countries, 113

ecological reality, 136
economic: greed, 132; growth,
    xi, 1, 149; recession, 8
education, 11, 14

166

Index

educational level of immigrants, 61
educational resources, 44, 125
El Paso, Texas, 100
elderly immigrants, 66
electoral votes in states with large
  Hispanic populations, 84
employer sanctions for hiring
  illegal immigrants, 27
employment discrimination, 96
Endangered Species Act, 6
energy consumption, 7
English as common language:
  dangers of weakening, 121; de
  Tocqueville declares importance
  of, 122; is wavering, 120; raises
  income of immigrants, 121
entry-level jobs, 135, 147
environment: air pollution, 10; loss
  of open space, 9, 12; physical,
  11, 149; psychic, 9, 11, 15, 149
Environmental Protection Agency
  (EPA), 4
ethnic composition, U.S. population, ix–x, 2; of California, 6
ethnic: labels, 129; leaders,
  130
ethnicity, should not be factor in
  immigration policy, 144
European Union, 138

family reunification: agenda of
  immigrant organizations, 26;
  central theme of U.S. policy,
  142; focused on instead of
  immigrants potential, 60–61;
  new focus of immigration policy, 21; objective of immigration
  program, 22; strategy of conservative Democrats, 55

family values, 62
farm labor force: 40 percent to 80
  illegal, 47, 70
fastest growing metro areas in
  U.S., 133
Federal Highway Administration,
  10
Fertility: excess, 134; of immigrants, 58–59
financial sponsor, 64
Florida: bi-lingual education
  began here, 122; has many
  Cuban and Colombian expatriates, 74, 88; Miami's huge
  Cuban population, 115; psychic
  hotspot, 15; quality of life
  diminished by Cubans, 115;
  sugarcane industry, 51–52,
foreign students, 11, 37–39,
  43–44
Fourteenth Amendment (to U.S.
  Constitution), 116
Fox, Vincente, 90–91
free market: allow it to determine
  labor costs, 148; crops in, 54;
  farm labor thwarts, 49; H-1B
  visas upset it, 35
fresh fruits and vegetables, portion
  of cost attributable to farm labor
  cost, 50
friction: social, xi; Koreans in California cause, 17; over Laotian
  Hmongs, 17

Gallegly Amendment, 31
genital mutilation, 73–74, 114
Gonzalez, Elian, 15
green card, 40, 48
group rights, 129–130, 132

Index

H-1B visas, 33–36, 39
hardship status, 82
hate crimes, 14
Hesburgh, Theodore, 57
high school drop-out rates compared, 19
higher education system, 43
high-tech industries: alternative to importing people, 42; curable shortage of workers, 43; lobby, 33
Hispanics: as source of immigrants, 2, 84; in Houston, 13; high school drop-out rate, 19; some support reduced immigration, 29
Hotel Employees and Restaurant Employees Union, 83–84
human rights violations, 80

I.B.M., 39
identification documents, employers required to verify, 28
illegal immigrants: abuse by smugglers, 93; agriculture's reliance on, 45; America not really serious about excluding, 82; amnesty for, 26; anger over, 31; better controlled after moratorium, 146; broker for, 95; California's cost of educating, 125–126; can't be denied public education, 31; deterrents to, 105; difficult existence of, 125; estimates of, 3, 96; percent Hispanic, 84; reasons they come, 104–105; sanctions for hiring, 69; their children are disadvantaged, 125; visa over-stayers are,

33; willing to work for any price, 49; wrong crops exploit, 54
Illegal Immigration Reform and Immigrant Responsibility Act, 104
immigrant entrepreneurship, 40–42
Immigration and Nationality Act: amendments to, 2, 21, 55; numerical limits embedded in, 24
immigration policy: importance of, 142–143
Immigration Reform and Control Act of 1986 (IRCA), 27, 46–48, 69, 82, 86
Immigration: how to decrease, 148; lawyers, 33; rate of, 5
income disparity, 147–148
India: a source for low cost technicians, 36; infanticide and caste-related violence in, 80
infrastructure, 7
initiative process, 143
Immigration and Naturalization Service (INS): backlog, 83; estimates 80 percent of asylum applicants stay in U.S., 77; Border Patrol, a division of, 92; issues fuzzy regulations, 64; need to research foreign cultures, 114; other agencies can't report fraud to, 97; substitutes binding contract, 67; unmasked phony, 76; why they don't pursue users of bad SS numbers, 72
intermarriage, 2
Internal Revenue Service (IRS), 97
Internet, 98

Index

job skills, as condition of immigration, 23

Kennedy, Edward M., (Ted), 2, 31

Lamm, Richard D., 5, 136
latchkey kids, 148
League of United Latin American Citizens (LULAC), 30
legal immigration: can be absorbed, 124; peak of, 3, 22; top source countries, 24
low-cost labor, 25

Matloff, Norman, 36
Meissner, Doris, 69
Mexican-American Legal Defense and Education Fund (MALDEF), 30
Mexico: U.S. border with, 102; government's responsibility, 106; has low individual income, 90; immigrants from are slow to naturalize 112; largest source of immigrants, 111, 103; minimum wage, 107; radio and TV from, 111; source of immigrants, legal and illegal, 106
Microsoft, 43
military bases as detention centers, 106
moratorium, 146–147
multiculturalism: Canadian attempts at,122; coalesced with diversity, 126–127; preached as alternative to assimilation, 127–128; psycho-babble about, 121; UCLA's commencements, a study in, 127
mysterious disappearances, 79

Nation of immigrants concept outmoded, 68–69, 132
National Council of La Raza (NCLR), 30
national priorities, 149
naturalization: decline in standards for, 120; Mexicans slowest in, 112; on brink of irrelevancy, 118
New York, 12,
New York City, 19
Nicaraguan Adjustment and Central American Relief Act (NACARA), 82, 86
Nisei Farmers League (NFL), 45
Nogales, Arizona, 100
nuclear family, 22, 57,

open borders, 87
opinion polls support reduced immigration, 29–30
opportunities for minorities, 44
overcrowding, urban, xi,

Ph. D. candidates, 37
Plyler vs. Doe, 31, 125
political opportunism, 132
population growth, 133–136
pro-immigration interest groups, 65
Proposition 187 (California), 30, death at the hands of Gray Davis, 31; objectives, 125
Proposition 227 ended bi-lingual education in California, 123
public charge, 64
public schools, 30
Puerto Rico, 91

quality of life: diminished by Cubans in Florida, 115;

Index

quality of life (*continued*)
diminished by heavy immigration, 11; overcrowding decreases, 149; reduction in, will be noticed during recession, 20,
Quebec's secessionist movement, 122, 139

race, should not be a factor in immigration, 144
racial balance in school admissions, 129
racial set-asides, 129
racism, ix, 130, 132
raisin harvest, 53
Refugee Act of 1989, 77
refugees, definition of, 73, 77, 81
Rice, Condoleezza, 81

San Diego, 100
San Joaquin Valley (California), 52
sending nation, 133–134
Sierra Club, 7
Silicon Valley, 40–41, 90
Simpson–Mazzoli Bill, 27, 85
Simpson, Alan, 31, 39
slavery, 18
Smith, Lamar, 30
smugglers, called "coyotes," 93, deaths attributed to, 94; fees rise, 95,
Social Security Administration windfall, 71–72
source countries for immigrants, 24
special agricultural workers (SAWs), 46–47

sugar cane harvesting in Florida, 51-52
Supplemental Security Income (SSI), 66–67
Supreme Court, U.S., 31

temporary farm work, 48
Texas: high immigration, 13; Brownsville, 100; El Paso, 100
tomato harvesting, 50–51
traffic, 8, 10
tribalism, 139

underclass, 1, 19, 146–147
United Nations High Commissioner for Refugees, 80
University of California at Berkeley, 38

Venezuela, 88–89
victimhood, 128
vigilante justice, 102
visa abusers, 3, 33, 91–92
voluntary return, (VR), 93
Voting Rights Act, 130

Washington, D.C., 13, 89
welfare: babies born to illegal parents in U.S., 117; elderly immigrant participation, 66; immigrants disproportionate participation, 61; non-cash participation, 65; refugees and asylees immediately eligible, 73
wet feet policy, 74–75

170